I0642115

Voltaire

Letters from M. de Voltaire, to Several of his Friends

Second Edition

Voltaire

Letters from M. de Voltaire, to Several of his Friends
Second Edition

ISBN/EAN: 9783744764056

Printed in Europe, USA, Canada, Australia, Japan

Cover: Foto ©Andreas Hilbeck / pixelio.de

More available books at **www.hansebooks.com**

LETTERS,

FROM

M. DE VOLTAIRE,

TO SEVERAL OF

HIS · FRIENDS.

TRANSLATED FROM THE FRENCH

BY THE REV. DR. FRANKLIN.

THE SECOND EDITION.

LONDON:

Printed for T. Davies, in Ruffel-Street, Covent-Garden.

MDCCLXXIII.

VOLTAIRE'S LETTERS.

L E T T E R * I.

To M. Le Chevalier de B R U A N T.

I WAS not at *** when your letter came; you embarrafs me greatly; I fhall only anfwer you for the pleafure of entertaining myfelf with a man who is much better able to refolve the doubts which he propofed, than the perfon to whom he fent them.

I am not of your opinion with regard to defpotifm and defpotic princes. It appears to me horrible and abfurd to the laft degree,

---

* The three firft letters are not Voltaire's, but fuppofed to be written by the celebrated author of L'Efprit des Loix, and feem worthy of him.

that a whole people fhould blindly fubject themfelves to the caprice of one, even if he were an angel. For my own part, I would not live under him a fingle day. This angel may become in a moment a monfter, thirfting after blood. Defpotifm is to me the moft abominable and difguftful of all bad governments; man is perpetually crufhed, debafed, and degraded by it. Look into hiftory, ancient and modern, if ever there was one upon earth that was not an infult on mankind, and the difgrace of human nature. Monarchy would doubtlefs be the beft of governments, if it was poffible to find fuch kings as Henry IV. the only one who ever deferved the homage and veneration of his fubjects. Kings fhould always be brought up in the fchool of affliction, as this great man was; fuch alone are truly great, and the lovers of mankind. Before we can feel for the misfortunes of others, we muft ourfelves have been unfortunate. But on the other hand, the hearts of princes, corrupted by profperity, and the flaves of pride and folly, are inacceffible to pity, and infenfible of true glory.

I am

. I am not at all furprifed, that in mo⸗ narchies, and efpecially in our own, there fhould be fo few princes worthy of efteem. Incircled by corruptors, knaves, and hypo- crites, they accuftom themfelves to look upon their fellow-creatures with difdain, and fet no value on any but the fycophants, who carefs their vices, and live in perpe- tual idlenefs and inactivity. Such is ge⸗ nerally the condition of a monarch; great men are always fcarce, and great kings ftill more fo. Add to this, that the fplendor of a monarchy is fhort and tranfitory. France is already funk into mifery and difgrace; an age more will annihilate her, or fhe will fall a prey to the firft intrepid con- queror.

The Englifh government has nothing to fupport it but a delufive outfide, extremely flattering to the people, who fanfy them- felves the fole governors. I do not know any country where it is more eafy to create fuch open diffentions as may overthrow the ftate. A man of fenfe and generofity may, in ten years time, erect himfelf into a defpotic prince with more fafety at London than at Mofkow: remember Cromwell. Money alone is fufficient to corrupt the whole parliament.

The great, ever fond of riches and power, and proftrate at the feet of fortune, who always attends the throne, will promote the views of their mafter; and the great once gained over, this fantom of liberty, which appeared at intervals in the convulfive motions of the commons, which awakens, fhakes itfelf, and foon vanifhes, will be totally annihilated at the firft fignal given by the fupreme ruler.

I know indeed of no monarchy that is fixed, conftant, and perfect; the wifeft kings opprefs their fubjects to arrive at defpotifm. Adieu, my friend; live in freedom and obfcurity. Solitude will procure you the beft and trueft pleafure, felf-content. The foolifh and the wicked feen afar off, will only excite your compaffion; to look nearly

upon

upon them, would raife your contempt and indignation.

I write this in hafte ; we will treat this matter more fully in the free intercourfe of guiltlefs friendfhip.

LET-

LETTER II.

YOU afk me in what country a man may enjoy the moft perfect liberty? In every place, my dear Philintus, where there are men and laws. The wife man is free even in the court of a tyrant, becaufe his happinefs depends on himfelf. Reafon and confcience are the throne of his liberty. It is not in the power of fortune, injuftice, or any thing elfe to unhinge his foul, or difturb his repofe. He rejoices in himfelf, and his joy is always calm, permanent, and delightful.

Would you, my friend, becaufe you fee violence and iniquity every day committed by wicked minifters, by the rich and great, by almoft every man in place and power; would you therefore intirely banifh yourfelf from that fociety to which you are indebted for every thing, and for which every honeft and good member of it fhould yield up all, without repining at the injuries which he

fuffers

fuffers from it ? Becaufe a prince buries himfelf in floth and debauchery ; becaufe he per-
fecutes, opprefles, and deftroys, fhall you
become an exile from your country, leave
your friends, and defert the poor and af-
flicted, who apply to you for relief, and rend
your heart with their complaints ? No, my
friend, you have too much fenfibility. Defpife the unjuft and cruel prince ; but love
mankind, and above all the unfortunate and
diftreffed. Avoid the impetuous whirlwinds
of a court ; forget, if poffible, that your
king is furrounded with perverfe, wicked,
and oppreffive men, who laugh at his ignorance, and avail themfelves of his weaknefs.
Fly to retirement, in fearch of that repofe,
friendfhip and felicity, which are never to
be found in the feats of power and grandeur, or in the dangerous and delufive
tumults of a noify metropolis. Bring with
you a few friends, as worthy and fenfible
as yourfelf. Read Plato, Montagne, Charron, and Rabelais ; exercife yourfelf in acts
of kindnefs to the poor labourers, the
only creatures upon earth who are always
miferable, perpetually toiling to fupply the

ne-

neceffities of nature, and victims to the cruel rapacity of the farmers-general, who grind and opprefs them.

Thus will you enjoy the moft delicate and lively of all pleafures, the pleafure of doing good, the only confolation that can reconcile us to the miferies of human life. When once you are habituated to a country life, joy and peace will revive in your difquieted and uneafy mind, which will grow ftrong and great, raifing itfelf by degrees to the celeftial regions of genius and philofophy. There, free as the air you breathe, throw out your thoughts as they arife; your foul will then fhoot forth fuch divine flames as fhall warm and enlighten even the cold and ignorant. When you have filled your paper, arrange and correct the whole, and I will tell you with the utmoft freedom my opinion of it. Adieu, my dear friend : with a heart of fuch delicate fenfibility as yours is, youth, health, and a tolerable fortune, you muft be happy, if happinefs is the portion of virtue.

L E T-

LETTER III.

YOU are right, my dear Philinthus, in believing and afferting to all your friends that education makes the man. That alone is the parent of every virtue ; it is the moft facred, the moft ufeful, and at the fame time the moft neglected thing in almoft every country, and in every ftation of life. But too many vague and impracticable rules have been laid down on this important fubject. Even the wife Locke, the great inftructor of mankind, is fometimes miftaken, like other writers. All education fhould have an eye to government, or we lofe our aim. The man of patience and underftanding will confider well the mind he has to form and inftruct ; he will infufe by little and little maxims adapted to his age, and fuited to his genius, rank, and capacity. I know that there are fome foils barren and ungrateful, and which will never anfwer the labour of the cultivator. But befides that fuch are very uncommon, I am in-

B 5   clined

clined to fufpect, that frequently the tiller
has neither strength nor skill enough to dig
into and improve it as he ought.

There is one radical vice in France,
which may perhaps never be extirpated,
becaufe it comes from the women, who,
amongst us, interfere in every thing, and
in the end ruin and destroy every thing.
A child is soon spoiled in their hands,
from two years old to fix, when he is delivered up, without confideration, to a man
whom he has neither feen nor known.
The tutor, perhaps a fellow of no character, takes charge of him, not from inclination, but merely for his own interest.
For ten fucceeding years he vegetates in
the narrow circle of a college, or in the
unimproving converfe and fociety of pra-
ting females of quality. Thefe tutors are
generally appointed by the women, who
feldom look any further than the outfide;
never confidering perfonal merit, which
they have not fenfe enough to diftinguish,
having never habituated themfelves to re-

ffect one moment on any thing ferious or
ufeful.

Another circumftance highly prejudicial
to education, and which difgufts and deters
men of merit from engaging in it, is the
little regard paid to the tutor or preceptor, who ought to be refpected as a father, whofe place he is in a great meafure intended to fupply : he to whom is intrufted the heir of an illuftrious name and
family; he who is to form the worthy citizen, and the good fubject; who is to do
honour to his rank and character, and become the glory of his country. Such are
the men, charged as they are with fo important an office, who, in the fafhionable
world, are fo often defpifed and ill-treated,
and even fometimes fuffered to perifh for
want. Such abufes, if they become general, muft point out a fhameful and univerfal depravity of manners. Our nobility indeed are free from this reproach ; if they
pay but indifferently, they make amends by
the weight of their intereft, and a thoufand engaging civilities, for the fmall ap-
pointment.

pointment which their fortune will permit them to allow. Your rich financiers, on the other hand, who are naturally morose, proud, and oftentatious, seldom pay a man without affronting him ; having nothing but money to give, they gorge you with it.

In France the women ruin every thing, because they think themselves fit for every thing, and the men are weak and childish enough to humour their caprice. Nature notwithstanding made them but to obey, and the weakness of their constitution every day points out to us the weakness of their sex. With regard to education, it is worse at court than in any other place ; the governor having a despotic power over his pupil, suffers him to grow up in ignorance and idleness, fills his head with the nonsence of fashion, and puffs him up with the notion of his own rank, and a contempt of the insignificant creatures that crawl beneath him. Every thing around him is to be made subservient to his pleasure or advancement. Every thing is to fall down before him on the first notice. He never talks to him concerning

cerning the royal virtues that adorn a throne, juſtice, courage, beneficence, intrepidity, and the love of glory; and therefore it is, that, amongſt our kings, we never fee a great man; for I call not the conqueror by that name, but rather confider him as the terror, fcourge, and difgrace of human-kind; one whom the people are bound by their own intereſt to deſtroy, as foon as the flame of his ambition breaks forth in projeĉts of ſlaughter and oppreſſion.

Lewis XII. was honeſt and juſt, but weak and ignorant. Francis I. a vain boaſter, cruel, and a pretender to wit. Henry IV. brave and magnanimous; but too much given to women ever to become a philofopher. Lewis XIV. at once the greateſt and meaneſt of mankind, would have excelled all the monarchs in the univerfe, if he had not been corrupted in his youth by bafe and ambitious flatterers. A ſlave during his whole life to pride and vain-glory, he never really boved his fubjeĉts, even for a moment; yet expeĉted at the fame time, like a true arbitrary prince, that they ſhould facrifice them-
ſelves

felves to his will and pleafure. Intoxicated with power and grandeur, he imagined the whole world was made but to promote his happinefs. He was feared, obeyed, idolized, hated, mortified, and abandoned. He lived like a fultan, and died like a woman. His reign was immortalized by the lowcft of his fubjects.

It is therefore, my dear Philinthus, impof-fible there fhould ever be a great man amongft our kings, who are made brutes and fools of all their lives, by a fet of infamous wretches, who furround and befet them from the cradle to the grave.

LET-

LETTERS

FROM

MR. VOLTAIRE.

LETTER I.

To M. L'Abbé D'OLIVET, Chancellor of the French Academy:

Ferney, Aug. 20. 1761.

YOU advised me, my dear chancellor, to write notes only on those pieces of Corneille which are in possession of the stage. This I suppose you did with a view of lightening my burden, and I acquiesced in it; not so much from idleness, as from the desire I had of gratifying the public with

more

more expedition? but I perceive that my retreat has afforded me greater leifure than I
imagined it would ; and having already com-
mented all the plays that are acted, find that
I have ftill time to make fome ufeful ob-
fervations on the reft.

There are fome curious anecdotes worth
knowing, particularly with regard to my remarks on the language. I find, for inftance,
feveral words grown obfolete amongft us,
and even totally forgotten, which our neighbours the Englifh make ufe of with fuccefs.
They have a term to fignify true comic
pleafantry, that gaiety and urbanity, thofe
natural fallies which efcape a man even
without his own confcioufnefs of them.
This idea they exprefs by the word * humour,

* The definition which Mr. Voltaire has here
given us of humour, confidered as a fpecies of wit,
feems to be a very imperfect one. Mr. Addifon
has indeed obferved (fee Spectator, N° 35.) that
it is much eafier to defcribe what is not 'humour
than what is, and very difficult to define it,
otherwife than as Cowley has done wit, by ne-
gatives. Mr. Addifon has likewife remarked, in
another place (Spectator, N9 616.) that ridicule
is

mour, which they pronounce *yûmour*, and which they imagine is poffeffed by them-felves alone, and that other nations have no term which fufficiently marks out this fpe-cies of wit: it is notwithftanding an old word in our language, and ufed in this fenfe in feveral of the comedies of Corneille. When I fay that this humour is a kind of urbanity, I apply myfelf only to the man of letters, who muft know how ftrangely we have wrefted the word * *urbanitas* to politenefs, though the Latin was certainly received at Rome in another fenfe, and meant precifely what the Englifh call humour: in this fenfe it is taken by Horace, when he fays,

Frontis ad urbanæ defcendi præmia;

and never in any other, in that fatire at-tributed to Petronius, and which fo many

is never more ftrong than when it is concealed in gravity : That true humour lies in the thought, and arifes from the reprefentation of images in odd circumftances, and uncommon lights.

* Te hominem non folum fapientem, verum etiam ut nunc loquimur, urbanum, fays Tully. And in another place, Homo facetus, inducis fer-monem facetum & urbanum.

tafbelefs

tafte!efs critics have afcribed to a conful of
that name.

The word *partie* (or part) is likewife to
be met with in Corneille's comedies, and
made to fignify wit : fuch a man has parts,
as the Englifh fay : the term is an excellent
one.   It is the property of man to have nothing but parts ; he has one fpecies of wit,
one kind of talent, but never poffeffes them
all together.   The word wit is too vague an
expreffion, and when they tell you fuch a
man has wit, you have a right to afk, of
what fort ?

How many words do we want now,
which had great energy and ftrength in
the time of Corneille, and how much have
we loft, either from mere negligence, or too
much delicacy ! A time or a rendezvous was
affigned or *appointed*; he who arrived at the
place agreed on, and did not meet with the
perfons who had made the promife, was * *difappointed.*

* It feems rather extraordinary that when Mr.
Voltaire was comparing the Englifh and French
words

appointed, We have no word at prefent
to exprefs the precife fituation of a man
who keeps his word whilft another breaks
it.

We have given up fome phrafes abfo‑
lutely neceffary, which the Englifh have
happily availed themfelves of: a ftreet or
path‑way, without a thoroughfare, was
very properly expreffed by the word *ncn‑
paffe,* or *impaffe,* which the Englifh have
imitated. We are forced now to make
ufe of that low and vulgar phrafe *cul‑
de‑fac,* which occurs fo often, and difgraces
the French language.

I fhould never have done with this ar‑
ticle, were I to enumerate all the happy
phrafes which we borrowed from the Ita‑
lians, and have fince loft: not that our
own language wants copioufnefs or energy,

words together, he fhould forget our word *dif‑
appoint,* and not obferve, as he has done with
regard to the word humour, that Mr. Corneille,
and other writers of that time, moft probably
took it from us.

but that it certainly might have more. What has robbed us of our moſt valuable ſtock is that heap of frivolous books which have lately appeared, written in the ſtile of common converſation, and ſtuffed with mo-diſh phraſes, and improper expreſſions. We are impoveriſhed by our abundance.

But I proceed to an article of more im-portance, and which has determined me to purſue my comments even to Pertharite. Amidſt theſe ruins we may find ſome hidden treaſures. Who would imagine, for exam-ple, that in Pertharite one ſhould diſcover the ſeeds of Pyrrhus and Andromache, or that Racine had borrowed from it the ſentiments, or even the expreſſion ? And yet nothing is more true or ſelf-evident. Grimoald, in Corneille, threatens Rodelind that he will deſtroy her child in the cradle, if ſhe will not conſent to marry him.

* Son ſort eſt en vos mains; aimer ou dedaigner, Le va faire périr, ou le faire régner.

* I have given the original as well as a tranſla-tion of theſe paſſages, that thoſe who underſtand
the

The choice is thine, to love or to defpife;
To give your fon a crown, or fee him perifh.

Pyrrhus fays exactly the fame thing in the
fame fituation:

Je vous le dis, il faut, ou périr ou régner.

I fay again, a crown or death await you.

Grimoald, in Corneille, is for punifh-
ing:

Sur ce fils innocent
La dureté d'un cœur fi peu reconnoiffant.

On the guiltlefs fon
The cruel mother's bafe ingratitude.

Pyrrhus fays, in Racine:

Le fils me repondra des mepris de la mere.

the French language may be better able to determine with regard to the propriety of Mr. Voltaire's
remarks on them.

2

The

The fon fhall anfwer for the mother's fcorn.

Rodelind fays to Grimoald :

Compte, penfes y bien, & pour m'avoir aimée
N'imprime point de tâche à tant de renommée.
Ne crois que ta virtu ; laiffe la feule agir,
De peur qu'un tel effort ne te donne à rougir ;
On publiroit de toi que le cœur d'une femme.
Plus que ta propre gloire, auroit touché ton
    ame ;
On diroit qu'un heros fi grand, fi renommé
Ne feroit qu'un tyrant, s'il n'avoit point aimé.

Think well on this, my lord, nor ftain a name
Unfpotted yet, with inhumanity.
Let virtue dictate, left you blufh hereafter,
When 'tis too late ; it will be faid, the heart
Of a weak woman had more pow'rful influence
Than fame or glory : that this hero, long
Renown'd in arms, had been a ruthlefs tyrant,
Had he not lov'd——

Andromache fays to Pyrrhus :

Seigneur, que faites vous, & que dira laGrece?
                              Faut

Faut il qu'un fi grand cœur montre tant de
  foiblefſe,
Et qu'un defſein fi beau, fi grand, fi genereux
Paſſe pour le tranfport d'un efprit amoureux ?
Non, non, d'un ennemi refpeĉter la mifere,
Sauver des malheureux, rendre un fils à fa
    mere,
De cent peuples pour lui combattre la rigueur,
Sans lui faire payer fon falut de mon cœur,
Malgré moi, fi'l le faut, lui donner un azile ;
Seigneur, voilà des foins dignes du fils d'Achille.

Confider, fir, how this will found in Greece!
How can fo great a foul betray fuch weaknefs?
Let not men fay fo gen'rous a defign.
Was but the tranfport of a heart in love.
                    PHILIPS's Diftrefs'd Mother.

The refemblance, you fee, runs through
the whole, and the imitation is apparent;
but I can tell you more, and what will
aftoniſh you : all the fcenes of Oreftes and
Hermione, at leaft the foundation of them,
are taken from Garibald and Enduige, two
obfcure charaĉters in this obfcure and
wretched piece ; fuch barbarous names alone
                              would

would have been fufficient to damn the play,
which Boileau vifibly alludes to, where he
fays,

Qui de tànt de heros va choifir Childebrand ?

Amidft fo many heroes, who would choofe
A Childebrand ?

But Garibald, all Garibald as he is, plays
exactly the fame part with Enduige as
Oreftes does with Hermione; Enduige loves
Grimoald, as Hermione does Pyrrhus; fhe
defires Garibald to revenge her of a traitor,
who quits her for Rodelind; as Hermione
requefts Oreftes to revenge her on Pyrrhus,
who deferts her for Andromache.

Enduige fays,

Pour gagner mon amour il faut fervir ma
hoine.

To gain my love you muft affift my hate.

Hermione

Hermione fays,

Vengez moi.   Je crois tout.

Avenge my wrongs, and I believe them all.
                              Diſtreſs'd Mother.

Geribald.

Le pourrez vous, madame ? & ſavez vous vos
    forces,
Savez vous de l'amour quelles ſont les
    amorces,
Savez vous ce qu'il peut, & qu'un viſage
    aimé
Eſt toujours trop aimable à ce qu'il a charmé ?
Si vous ne m'abuſez, votre cœur vous abuſe, &c.

And can you, madam ! Know you your own
    heart ?
Know you the ſtrong deluſive pow'r of love ?
Know you the face ſhe once admir'd is ſtill
Moſt beauteous in a doting woman's eye ?
If you deceive not me, you are deceiv'd
By your own heart——

             C   Oreſtes,

Oreftes.

Et vous le haiffez ? Avouez le, madame ;
L'amour n'eft pas un feu qu'on enferme en
    une aime ;
Tout nous trahit ; la voix, le filence, les
    yeux ;
Et les feux mal couverts n'en eclatent que
    mieux.

You hate him then : alas ! the flames of love
Are not fo foon extinguifh'd or conceal'd.
Our looks, our words, nay ev'n our filence oft
Betrays us ; and the fire that's fmother'd o'er
Breaks out afrefh, and only burns the fiercer.

Thefe ideas which the genius of Corneille
threw out by chance, without improving on
them, the tafte of Racine gathered up, and
formed into a complete work ; he picked out
out the gold *de ftercore Ennii.*

Corneille never confulted any friend,
whilft Racine took the advice of Boileau ;
and for this reafon the former, from the publication of Heraclius, always declined ; the
latter

latter rofe every day into higher reputation.
It is generally believed that Racine enervated
and difgraced the ftage by the love fcenes
which he perpetually brought upon it; but
truth obliges me to acknowledge, that Corneille, and before him Rotrou, were guilty
of the fame fault.

There is not one of their pieces which is
not, partly at leaft, founded on this paffion ;
the only difference is, that they never treated
it properly, never fpoke to the heart, or
made any impreffion on it. Their love was
never affecting, except in thofe fcenes of the
Cid, which are taken from the Guillain of
de Caftro. Corneille introduced love even
into the terrible fubject of Œdipus, which
you may remember I was bold enough to
attempt about feven and forty years ago. I
have now by me a letter from Mr. Dacier in
1714, to whom I fhewed my third act, imitated from Sophocles, wherein he advifes me
to reftore the ancient chorus, and by no
means to talk of love in a fubject fo ill
adapted to it. I followed his advice, and
read my piece to the comedians, who infifted

on

on my withdrawing part of the chorus, and at leaft bringing in fome remembrance of love in the part of Philoctetes; that his fentiments might make fome amends, they faid, for the infipidity of Œdipus and Jocafta.

Even the little part of the chorus which I retained was never fpoken. Such was the horrid tafte of thofe times. Some years after, Athaliah, that mafter-piece of dramatic writing, was exhibited; the nation might have learned from thence that the ftage could fubfift without that fpecies of dialogue which fo often degenerates into eclogues and idylliums. But as Athaliah was fupported by the pathos of religion, they imagined there was a neceffity for love in all prophane fubjects.

At length Merope and Oreftes have opened the eyes of the public. I am fatisfied the author of Electra muft think as I do in this refpect, and that he would never have introduced two love intrigues into the moft fublime and awful fubject of antiquity, if he had not

been

been obliged to it by the wretched cuftom
eftablifhed of disfiguring every thing by thefe
fafhionable puerilities: the ridicule of it
was at laft found out, and the cuftom ex-
ploded.

Strangers laughed at us for a long time, but
we knew nothing of it; we imagined it was
impoffible for a woman to appear on the ftage
without faying I love, a hundred different
ways, and in verfes loaded with botching
epithets. Nothing was heard but * flamme
and ame, feux and veux, cœur and vainqueur.
But Corneille rofe far above thefe trifles in
his Horace, Cinna, Pompey, &c. all his
pieces will furnifh me with entertaining
anecdotes, and interefting reflections. Do
not be furprifed if my commentaries fhould
fwell into as many volumes as your Cicero.
Prevail on the academy to continue its kind
protection to me, and its inftructions, and

* Flame, foul, fires, vows, heart, conqueror;
thefe don't rhime in Englifh, and therefore could
not be tranflated: if the author had written in
our tongue he would have faid, fire, defire, arms,
charms, &c.

above

' above all affift it with your own example.
The bookfellers of Geneva who have undertaken this edition by confent of the company, affure me that nothing was ever publifhed at fo low a price; it is neceffary indeed
that it fhould be fo, that thofe whofe fortune is not equal to their tafte and knowledge, may enjoy the benefit of it. It is intended to be made a prefent of to thofe who
are not in a capacity to purchafe it : works
are generally given to the rich and great,
though the contrary ought moft certainly to
take place, which is with regard to this
edition, the intention of fome of the moft
confiderable perfons in the nation, who make
it a point to pay all poffible honours to the
great Corneille, almoft a hundred years after
his death, and in the worft of times.

Our literary hiftory cannot furnifh us with an
example of any thing fo extraordinary as what
has happened in regard to this affair. Two perfons whom I never had the honour of feeing,
whom I never fo much as wrote to or
folicited, volutarily undertook the tafk with
that

that zeal and alacrity, without which it could not poffibly have fucceeded.

One of them is the dutchefs of Gramont, who warmly patronifed the fcheme, prevailed on a confiderable number of foreigners to fubfcribe to it, and who, in fhort, merely from generofity and greatnefs of foul, has done for Mr. Corneille, though an utter ftranger to her, every thing which could have been expected from a moft intimate friend and acquaintance. I affure you the fineft pieces of the great Corneille himfelf never affected me more than this incident.

Our other benefactor, would you believe it? is the court Banker, Mr. Delaborde, who, without any knowledge of me, or acquainting me with his intention, procured above a hundred fubfcriptions, which we never even heard of here till after it was done. Thus generoufly fupported and encouraged, I took the liberty to addrefs the king, our great protector, to permit his name to be placed at the head of the fubfcription : I flattered myfelf he would condefcend to take fifty

copies;

copies; he took two hundred. I applied for a dozen from his royal highnefs the infant duke of Parma, he fubfcribed for thirty. Almoft all the princes of the blood gave us their names. The duke of Choifeul fet himfelf down for twenty; the marchionefs of Pompadour, to whom I had not fo much as written, took fifty, her brother twelve. Amongft the members of our academy, the count Clermont, cardinal de Bernes, marfhal Richelieu, and the duke of Nivernois diftinguifhed themfelves.

Mr. Watelet not only takes five copies, but is fo good as to defign and grave the frontifpiece, affifting us both with his genius and his purfe. But what will you fay when I tell you that Mr. Bóuret, whom I fcarce know, has fubfcribed for four and twenty?

All this was done before any notice was given of printing it, and before it was known what would be the price of it. The company of farmers-general fubfcribed for fixty, and feveral other focieties have followed their example. This noble emulation becomes

comes general : fcarce was the firft report of this edition fpread in Germany, before the elector palatine, and the dutchefs of Saxegotha exerted themfelves in favour of it. At London we have my lord Chefterfield, lord Middleton, Mr. Fox the fecretary of ftate, the duke of Gordon, Mr. Crawford, and feveral others.

You fee, my dear brother, how, whilft politics divide kingdoms, and fanaticifm feparates fellow-citizens, the belles letters reunite them : what can reflect more honour and praife on the polite arts ? As much as men defpife and contemn thofe who difgrace literature by their infamous periodical abufe, and thofe alfo who perfecute and opprefs it, fo much do they refpect and honour Corneille in every part of Europe.

The bookfellers of Geneva who have undertaken this edition, enter generoufly into the defign of it. They are of a family who many years have been in the council ; one of them is a member. They are in fhort men who think as they ought to think, and confult not

C 5 their

their intereft but their reputation. They will receive no money from any one till after the delivery of the firft volume ; and give twelve or thirteen volumes in octavo, with three and thirty fine prints for two louifd'ors : a great deal muft certainly be loft by this, it could not be done therefore by way of precaution to fecure the fale of the copies ; it was abfolutely neceffary, and without the benefactions of the king, and the generofity of thofe who affifted, the fcheme, like many other projects, would have been firft approved of, and then fallen to the ground.

I afk pardon for the length of my letter, but commentators never know when to leave off, and yet generally fay very little to the purpofe.

If you have a mind I fhould fay good things, write to me, &c.

LET-

LETTER II.

Mr. VOLTAIRE's Anſwer to the Duke of BOUILLON, who had written him a Letter in Verſe, on the Edition of CORNEILLE, publiſhed by him for the Benefit of the Niece of that great Man.

YOU are like the marquis de la Farre, my lord, who began to diſcover his genius for poetry at about your age, when ſome certain more valuable talents ſeemed to decline, and to acquaint him that there were other pleaſures reſerved for him. His firſt verſes were dedicated to love; his ſecond to the abbé Chaulieu. Your firſt fruits were offered to me. This, my lord, was not altogether juſt; but I am the more obliged to you for it. You tell me, I have always triumphed over my enemies; to you I am indebted for my greateſt triumph.

'Midſt

'Midſt barren rocks the heedleſs poet plays,
Whilſt Corneille's daughter liſtens to his.
    lays,
Nor ſhall regret thy banks, delightful Seine,
Whilſt he is prais'd and ſung by great
    Turenne.
There ever is a kind retreat for me,
Or with Bellona, or Melpomene ;
Favour'd by theſe, and ſuch as theſe alone,
I laugh at folly, malice, and Freron.
'Tis double joy, and makes our bliſs complete,
To ſee pale envy proſtrate at our feet,
To brave the rav'nous harpies, thus releas'd
From danger, gives new reliſh to the feaſt ;
And clam'rous * Berthier's calumnies to me,
At diſtance heard, are pleaſant harmony.

How ſweet it is, whilſt in my Chloe's arms
Content I ſit, enraptur'd with her charms,
To write, inſpir'd by my ſuperior ſtate,
A ſatire on my wretched rival's fate,

* The French edition of theſe letters informs
us, in a note, that this Berthier was formerly a
Jeſuit, the profeſſed enemy of genius and literature ; a kind of ſpy, employed by ſome devotees
of the court, from whom he received penſions.

To

To make the whining fool in all fubmit,
And envy both the lover and the wit.

But this, you'll fay, is not a Chriftian's part,
To rail and perfecute : with all my heart;
I grant, my lord, the pow'rful plea; but then
You'll own with me that Chriftians are but
    men :
The world's a ftate of warfare, and we know,
In ev'ry place hath ev'ry man a foe.
'Midft mortals here eternal quarrels rife ;
Nay, we have heard of battles in the fkies.
The court, the army, and the church have
    fought
For wealth, for pow'r, for fomething, and for
    nought ;
Ev'n fair Parnaffus, to Parnaffus' fhame,
Hath fought with ardour for an empty name.

We fit above, my friend, who better know,
And laugh at all the little crowd below.

Laughers as we are, my lord, we may ftill
be doing good. Your lordfhip I am fure will
to Mrs. Corneille. You have defired me to
tax you for as many copies as I pleafe. If I
                       consulted

confulted your heart only, I fhould rate you like the king, and put you down for two hundred ; but as I know you are perpetually fcattering your money abroad in every place, till fometimes you are left without a fhilling, I fhall reduce you to fix, and increafe the number as foon as I find you are turned oeconomift.

I befeech your highnefs to preferve your regard for your poor Swifs,

VOLTAIRE.

L E T T E R III.

To the Duke of V.A L I E R E, Grand Falconer.

YOU refemble, my lord, the heroes of ancient chivalry, by thus expofing your own perfon in defence of your faithful followers, when in danger ; but the little error which you led me into has been the means of difplaying your profound erudition. Few grand falconers would have delivered the *Sermones Fefivi*, printed in 1502. Raillery apart, to put yourfelf in the breach for me, was an action worthy of your noble heart.

You told me, in your firft letter, that Urceus Codrus was a great preacher ; your fecond informs me he was a great libertine, but no cordelier. You afk pardon of St. Francis and all the feraphic order, for the contempt into which I am fallen. I join with you, and put on my penitentials ; but it ftill

re-

remains true, that the myfteries reprefented at the Hotel de Bourgogne were more decent than moft of our modern fermons. Place who we pleafe in the room of Urceus Codrus, and we fhall yet be in the right. There is not a word in the myfteries offenfive to piety and good manners. Forty people would never agree to write and act facred poems in French, that fhould difguft the public by their indecency, and of courfe oblige them to fhut up their doors. But an ignorant preacher, who works by himfelf, and is accountable to none for what he does, who has no idea of decorum, may very probably advance fome ridiculous things in his fermon, efpecially when he delivers it in Latin. Such, for inftance, are the difcourfes of the cordelier Maillard, which you undoubtedly have in your large and valuable collection ; in his fermon on the Thurfday in the fecond week of Lent, he addreffes himfelf thus to the lawyers wives that wore gowns embroidered with gold.

" You fay you are cloathed according to " rank; go to the devil, ladies, you and " your rank together. You will tell me,

" per-

" perhaps, our hufbands don't give us thefe
" fine gowns; we earn them by the induftry
" of our own fweet bodies : thirty thoufand
" devils take your induftry, and your bodies
" too."

I will not put you to the blufh, by quoting
any more paffages from brother Maillard;
but if you will take the trouble to look into
him, you will find fome ftrokes worthy of
Urceus Codrus. Brother Andrew and Mi-
not were likewife famous for their filthinefs.
The Pulpit was not indeed always polluted
by obfcenity; but for a long time fermons
were little better than the myfteries of the
Hotel de Bourgogne.

It muft be acknowledged, that the members of what they call the reformed church
in France, were the firft that brought reafon-
ing and argument into their difcourfes.
When we want to change the ideas, and al-
ter the principles of men, we muft make ufe
of reafon; but this was ftill very far from
eloquence. The pulpit, the bar, the ftage,
philofophy, literature, theology, every thing
we

we could boaſt of in thoſe times, ſome few particulars excepted, were beneath the common pieces exhibited at a country fair.

True taſte was not eſtabliſhed amongſt us till the reign of Lewis XIV. It was this which long ſince determined me to attempt a ſlight ſketch of that glorious æra; and you muſt have obſerved, in that hiſtory, the age is my hero more than Lewis himſelf, what reſpect and gratitude ſoever may be due to his memory.

It is true indeed, that, in general, our neighbours made no greater figures than ourſelves. How happened it that men could preach for ever, and yet preach ſo badly! and that the Italians, who had ſo long before ſhook off their barbarity in other reſpects, with regard to the pulpit were but ſo many harlequins with ſurplices on! Whilſt at the ſame time the Jeruſalem of Taſſo rival'd the Iliad, and Orlando Furioſo ſurpaſſed the Odyſſey; Paſtor Fido had no model in all antiquity, and Raphael and Paul Veroneſe actually

actually performed what was only imagined of Zeuxis and Apelles.

You muft certainly, my lord, have read the council of Trent. There is not a peer in the kingdom, I fuppofe, who does not perufe fome part of it every morning. You remember the fermon at the opening of the council by the bifhop of Bitonto.

He proves, firft, that the council is necef-fary, becaufe feveral councils have depofed kings and emperors. Secondly, becaufe, in the Æneid, Jupiter affembles a council of the gods. Thirdly, becaufe, at the creation of man, and the building of Babel, God at-tended to it in the manner of a council. He infifts on it, a little after, that the council fhould reduce themfelves to thirty, like the heroes in the Trojan horfe. And, finally, afferts, that the gate of Paradife and the gate of the council was the fame thing. That living water flowed from it, with which the holy fathers fhould fprinkle their hearts, which were as dry lands; or, in lieu of·this,

that

that the Holy Ghoft would open their mouths like the mouths of Balaam and Caiphas.

This, my lord, was preached before all the general ftates of Chriftendom. The fermon of St. Antony of Padua to the fifh is ftill more famous in Italy than that of the bifhop of Bitonto; we may excufe, therefore, our brother Andrew, brother Garaffe, and all the Giles's of our pulpits in the fixteenth and feventeenth centuries, as they were but on a level with our mafters the Italians. What could be the caufe of this grofs ignorance, fo univerfally fpread over Italy in the time of Taffo; over France in the days of Montagne, Charron, and the chancellor de l'Hofpital; and over England in the age of Bacon ? How happened it that thefe men of genius did not reform the times they lived in ? We muft attribute it to the colleges where youth were educated ; to that monkifh theologic fpirit which finifhed the barbarifm that the colleges had introduced. A genius, as Taffo was, read Virgil, and produced the Jerufalem. A merchant read Terence, and wrote Mandragora ; but what monk or curate,

rate, at that time of day, read Tully or Demofthenes ? A poor and wretched fcholar,
grown half an ideot by being obliged, for
four years together, to get John Defpautere
by heart; and half a madman by fupporting
a thefis *de rebus & partibus,* on thoughts and
categories, received his cap, and his letters
of recommendation, and away he went to
preach to an audience, three parts of whom
were greater fools, and worfe educated than
himfelf.

The people liftened to thefe theological
farces with outftretched necks, fixed eyes,
and open mouths, as children do to ftories of
witches and apparitions, and returned home
perfect penitents. The fame fpirit that made
them give ear to the nonfenfe of a foolifh mother, led them to thefe fermons; which they
attended the more diligently, as it coft them
nothing. It was not till the time of Coef-
feteau and Balzac that fome preachers began
to talk rationally; though at the fame time
they were very tirefome. Bourdaloue, in
fhort, was the firft man of any eloquence in
the pulpit. Of this, Burnet, bifhop of Salif-
bury,

bury, bears teſtimony, in his Memoirs ; where he tells us, that, in travelling through France, he was aſtoniſhed at his ſermons ; and that Bourdaloue reformed the preachers of England, as well as thoſe of France.

Bourdaloue might be ſtiled almoſt the Corneille of the pulpit, as Maſſillon became afterwards the Racine of it. Not that I mean to compare an art, half profane, to a miniſtry well-nigh holy ; nor, on the other hand, the little difficulty of making a good ſermon to the great and inexpreſſible one of compoſing a good tragedy. I only ſay, that Bourdaloue carried the art of reaſoning as far in preaching as Corneille did in the drama ; and that Maſſillon ſtudied to be as elegant in proſe, as Racine was in verſe. True indeed it is, that Bourdaloue was reproached, as well as Corneille, for being too much of a lawyer, for preferring argument to paſſion, and ſometimes producing but indifferent proofs. Maſſillon, on the other hand, choſe rather to paint, than to affect ; he imitated Racine as much as it was poſſible to do it in proſe ; not forgetting, at the

ſame

fame time, boldly to affert, that all dramatic authors would be damned. Every quack, you know, muft cry up his own noftrum, and condemn thofe of others. His ftile is pure; his defcriptions moving and pathetic. Read over this paffage on the humanity of the great.

" Alas! if any of us have an excufe for
" being morofe, whimfical, and melancholy,
" a burthen to ourfelves and all about us,. it
" muft be thofe miferable wretches, whom
" misfortunes, calamities, home-felt necef-
" fity, and gloomy cares perpetually fur-
" round. They might be forgiven, if with
" mourning, bitternefs, and defpair already
" in their hearts, the marks of it fhould
" fometimes appear in their external be-
" haviour. But fhall the great and happy
" of this world, whom joy and pleafure ac-
" company, whilft every thing fmiles around
" them; fhall thefe pretend to derive, even
" from their felicity, an excufe for their
" churlifhnefs and caprice? Shall they be
" melancholy, difquieted, and unfociable,
" becaufe they are more happy? Shall they
" look

" look upon it as the privilege of profpe-
" rity to opprefs with the weight of their
" ill humour the poor and unfortunate, who
" already groan beneath the yoke of their
" power and authority ?"

Recollect, at the fame time, thefe lines in
Britannicus :

Tout ce que vous voyez confpire à vos defirs
Vos jours toujours ferins coulent dans les
    plaifirs
L'empire en eft pour vous l'inépuifable fource,
Ou fi quelque chagrin en interrompt la courfe,
Tout l'univers, foignant de les entretenir
S'empreffe a l'effacer de votre fouvenir.
Britannicus eft feul, quelqu' ennui qui le
    preffe,
Il ne voit dans fon fort que moi qui l'intereffe,
Et n'a pour tous plaifirs, feigneur, que quel-
    ques pleurs
Qui lui font quelquefois oublier fes malheurs.

Whate'er thou feeft confpires to make thee
    happy,
Serene thy days in endlefs pleafures flow,

For

From the wide empire's unexhaufted fpring ;
Or if intruding forrow, for a while, ·
Breaks in upon thy joys, the world itfelf,
Still anxious for thy good, with ardour ftrives
To blot out every painful fad idea,
And give thee peace again. —Britannicus,
Mean time, is left alone; when cares opprefs,
I, only I, participate his griefs,
And all his comfort is the tears I fhed,
Which fometimes makes the wretch forget
    his forrows.

In comparing thefe two paffages together,
I perceive the fcholar, as it were, contending
with his mafter. I could fhew you twenty
more examples of the fame nature, but that
I am afraid of being tedious.

Maffillon and Cheminais knew Racine by
heart, and difguifed the verfes of that divine
poet in their pious profe. In the fame manner feveral preachers learned the art of declamation from Baron, and corrected the
gefture of the comedian by that of the facred
orator. Nothing can be a ftronger proof than
this, that the arts at leaft are brothers, though

the

the artifts themfelves are far from being
fo.

The worft of fermons is, that they are
only fo many declamations pro and con.
The fame man who affirmed laft Sunday
that there was no felicity in grandeur, that
crowns are thorns, that courts are full of
nothing but illuftrious wretches, and that
joy is fpred over the faces of the poor, will
tell you, the Sunday after, that the lower
part of mankind is condemned to mifery and
forrow; and that the rich and great muft one
day pay for their dangerous profperity.

They will inform you, in Advent, that
God is perpetually employed in removing all
the wants and neceffities of mankind; and,
when Lent comes, affure you, that the earth
is barren and accurfed. Thefe common
places, with a few flourifhing phrafes, carry
them on from one end of the year to the
other.

The preachers in England follow another
method, which would not fuit us at all.

The

The deepeft book of * metaphyfics which they have is Clarke's fermons : one would imagine he had preached only to philofo-phers, who perhaps too, at the end of every period, might have required of him a long explanation ; and the *Frenchman at London*, *to whom nothing could be proved*, would foon have left the preacher there. His dif-courfes, however, make an excellent book, which very few underftand. What a diffe-rence there is between ages and nations ! and how far off are brother Garaffe and brother Andrew from Maffillon and Clarke !

From my ftudy of hiftory I have at leaft learned, that the times we live in are cer-tainly of all times the moft enlightened, in fpite of our bad books, as they are alfo the moft happy, in fpite of fome cafual misfor-tunes : for what man of letters can be igno-rant that good tafte was brought into France

---

* Clarke's fermons are by no means, as Mr. Vol-taire here afferts, all metaphyfical : thofe indeed on the being of a God, &c. are certainly fo ; but there are withal as many excellent, plain, practical difcourfes in this collection, as in any of our beft writers.

about

about the time of Cinna, and the *Provincial
Letters!* or where is he, who has any knowledge of hiftory, that can point out a period
of time, from the days of Clovis, more
happy than what has paffed fince the Æra
when Louis XIV. began to reign by himfelf, down to the prefent moment? I defy
the moft malevolent to tell me what age he
would prefer to our own.

We muft do juftice; we muft acknowledge
that, at prefent, a geometrician of four-and-
twenty knows more than ever Defcartes did;
and that a country vicar preaches more fen-
fibly than the grand almoner of Louis XII.
The nation is better inftructed, our ftile
in general is much improved, and confequently the minds of men greatly fuperior
now to what they were formerly.

You will fay, perhaps, that our age is at
prefent on the decline, and that we have not
fo much genius and abilities amongft us as
we had in the glorious days of Louis XIV.
Genius, I grant you, decays; but know-
edge is increafed. A thoufand painters, in
the

the time of Salvator Rofa, were not worth a Raphael, or a Michael Angelo; but the thoufand painters formed by Raphael and Michael Angelo compofed a fchool infinitely fuperior to that which thofe two great men found eftablifhed. We have not, indeed, at the clofe of our fine age, a Maffillon, or a Bourdaloue, a Boffuet, or a Fenelon ; but the pooreft of our prefent preachers is a Demofthenes, in comparifon with all thofe who preached from the times of St. Remi to thofe of brother Garaffe.

There is more difference between the worft of our modern tragedies and the pieces of Jodelle, than between the Athaliah of Racine and the Maccabees of La Motte, or the Mofes of the abbé Nadal. Upon the whole, in the productions of the mind our artifts fall fhort of thofe who flourifhed in the dawn and meridian of our golden age; but the nation itfelf is improved. We are over-run indeed with trifles, and mine are always adding to the number: thefe are but fo many infects, which denote the abundance of fruits and flowers; you fee none of them in a barren foil. You will obferve, that in thefe little pieces that are perpetually coming out, deftroyed one by another, and all of them, in a few days, condemn'd to eternal oblivion, there is often more tafte and delicacy than you will find in all the books written before the *Provincial Letters*. Such is our affluence in wit, when compared to the poverty of twelve hundred years paft.

If you examine into the prefent ftate of our manners, laws, government, and fociety, you will find my accompt ftrictly juft. I date from the moment Lewis XIV. took the reins into his own hand, and would afk the moft exafperated critic, the graveft panegyrift of times paft, whether he durft compare the prefent period with that when the archbifhop of Paris went to parliament with a poignard in his pocket ? Or would he prefer the preceding age, when the firft minifter was fhot, and his wife condemned to be burned for a witch ? Ten or twelve years of the great Henry IV. appear happy, after forty of abominations and horrors, that make one's hair ftand an end ; but whilft the beft

of

of princes was employed in healing our
wounds, they bled on every fide. The poi-
fon of the league infected every mind; families were divided; the manners of men
harfh and difagreeable. Fanaticifm reigned
univerfally, except at the court. Commerce,
indeed, began to increafe; but was not, as
yet, attended with any great advantages.
Society had no charms, our cities no police;
all the comforts, in fhort, and conveniences
of life were ftill wanting. Figure to yourfelf, at the fame time, a hundred thoufand
affaffinations committed in the name of God.
Amidft the ruins of cities laid in afhes, even
to the time of Francis I. you will fee
Italy ftained with our blood, a king prifoner
at Madrid, and the enemy in the midft of our
provinces.

The name of *Pater Patriæ* was given to
Lewis XII. but this father had fome very unfortunate children, and was fo himfelf:
driven out of Italy, duped by the pope,
conquered by Henry VIII. and obliged to
bribe him to marry his fifter. He was a
good king, over a poor uncultivated people,

D. 4   without

without arts or manufacture; the houfes of his capital built with lath and plaifter, and moft of them covered with thatch. Who would not rather wifh to live under a good king, over a people opulent and wife, though dogmatical and mifchievous?

The further you go back into former ages, the more favage you will find them; which renders our hiftory fo difguftful, that we have been forced to make chronological abridgments in columns, where every thing neceffary is inferted, and only that which is ufelefs omitted, for the fake of thofe curious readers who are defirous of knowing in what year the Sorbonne was founded, and are in doubt whether the equeftrian ftatue in the Gothic cathedral at Paris is of Philip of Valois or Philip the Fair.

To fay the truth, we have not really and properly exifted above fix fcore years. Laws, police, military difcipline, trade, navigation, the fine arts, magnificence, tafte, and genius, all began in the time of Lewis XIV. Some of them are ripening to perfection in

our

our own age, which I meant to infinuate, when I advanced, that every thing heretofore was rude and barbarous, and the pulpit amongft them. Urceus Codrus moft certainly was not worth talking fo long about; but he has furnifhed me with reflections which may not perhaps be intirely ufelefs; we fhould endeavour to draw fome advantage from every thing.

LET.

LETTER IV.

To my Lord LYTTLETON, at
London.

I HAVE read the ingenious Dialogues of
the Dead, lately publifhed by your lordfhip,
where I find myfelf fpoken of as a banifhed
man, and guilty of many exceffes in my
writings. I am obliged, perhaps, for the
honour of my country, publicly to declare,
that I never was banifhed, becaufe I never
committed thofe crimes which the author of
the Dialogues has thought fit to lay to my
charge.

No man ever exerted himfelf more ftre-
nuoufly than myfelf in favour of the rights
of humanity, and yet never have I gone beyond the bounds of that virtue. I am not
eftablifhed in Swifferland, as this author,
who has been mifinformed, ventures to affert. I live on my own eftate in France.
Retirement is fit for old men, who have

lived

lived long enough in courts to detest and avoid them, and who enjoys new life in a peaceable retreat, with a few fenfible and faithful friends. I have indeed a little country houfe near Geneva ; but my refidence and feat are in Burgundy. The king's goodnefs to me, all the privileges belonging to my eftate, and the exemption of it from all taxes, has moreover firmly attached me to his perfon. If I had been banifhed, I could not have procured paffports from our court for feveral of the Englifh nobility. The fervice which I did them gives me a claim to that juftice which I expect from the author of the Dialogues.

With regard to religion, I think, and I believe he thinks fo too, that God is neither Prefbyterian nor Lutheran, high or low church, but the father of all mankind, of lord Littleton, and of

VOLTAIRE.

From the caftle of Ferney,
in Burgundy.

LETTER V.

To the Abbé T R U B L E T, who had
sent him his discourse on his being admitted a Member of the French Academy.

Chateau de Ferney, 27 April, 1761.

YOUR letter, Sir, together with your
generous manner of acting, prove that you
are not my enemy; though, by your book,
I should have suspected you of being so. I
had much rather give credit to your letter
than to your book. You have said in print,
that I made you yawn; and I have said in
print, that I laughed at it. It only follows from
hence, that you are not easily diverted, and
that I am a bad joker. Upon the whole,
both in yawning and in laughing you keep
me company! and we must forget every
thing like good Christians, and good Aca-
demicians.

I like

I like your difcourfe extremely well, and am obliged to you for fending it me; as to your letter,

> *Nardi parvus Onyx*
> *Elicitt cadum.*

I beg pardon for quoting Horace, which your heroes Fontenelle and la Motte never did; and muft tell you, that I was not born with more malice in my heart than yourfelf, and am at the bottom an honeft fellow.. It is true indeed, that having, fome years ago, taken it into my head that one got no-thing by being fo, I grew a little gay, be-caufe they faid it would be good for my health. Befides that I did not think my-felf fo confiderable and important as always to difdain certain illuftrious enemies, who attacked me perfonally for the fpace of forty years, and who one after another feemed re-folved on my deftruction, and perfecuted me with as much zeal as if I had contended with them for a bifhopric, or the place of a farmer-general. I fell upon them, at laft, out of pure modefty, and actually believed

myfelf

myfelf upon a level with them; as Tully
fays,

In arenam cum æqualibus defcendi.

Believe me, Sir, I make a great difference
between you and them; but I well remember, when I was at Paris, both my rivals
and myfelf were people of very little confequence; poor fcholars of the age of Lewis
XIV. fome in verfe, fome in profe, fome
half one and half the other (of which number I had the honour to be one) indefati-
gable writers of very middling performances,
great compofers of trifles, weighing moft
gravely the eggs of flies in fcales of fpiders
webs. I faw fcarce any thing but a little
quackery, and am perfectly convinced of the
nothingnefs of my own writings; but as I
equally perceive the nothingnefs of all the
reft, I imitate the Vejanius of Horace,

Vejanius, armis
Herculis ad poftem fixis, latet abditus agro.

It

It is from this retreat, I now assure you,
with the greatest sincerity, that I find a
great many useful and agreeable things in
what you have wrote: that I most cor-
dially forgive the pinches I have received
from you, and am sorry for the little scratches
which I have given you: that your manner
of proceeding has for ever disarmed my re-
sentment: that good-nature is better than
raillery: and that I am, my dear brother,
with the truest esteem, and without a compliment, as if nothing had happened between
us, with all my heart, yours, &c.

LETTER VI.

EPISTLE to SOPHIA.

IN Rome of old, as ancient poets sing,
And I believe, dame Flora was the thing;
Dictators, heroes, consuls, all the crowd
Of Glory's fav'rites at her altars bow'd;
The rich, the poor, the giddy, and the grave,
Or prince, or peasant, proud to be her slave:
With Cupids then the Roman eagles play'd,
And sported with her in the classic shade;
Crown'd by the gen'ral voice the queen of
 flow'rs,
In festive mirth she led the jocund hours;
For many an age she kept th' imperial seat,
And saw the world's proud conqu'rors at her
 feet.
At length her reign is o'er, the time is come,
When Paris in her queen shall rival Rome.
At length to thee, Sophia, nymph divine,
Her crown the vanquish'd Flora shall resign;
The joyful news to ev'ry zephyr known,
They welcome their new Flora to the throne.

In crowds the willing flaves obfequious ftand,
And waft their fpicy odours thro' the land.
The lover's month, 'fweet rofy-finger'd May,
Shall hail with dimpled fmiles th' aufpicious
    day;
Whilft fair Vertumnus, leader of the year,
The God of fpring, fhall in her train ap-
    pear.
Fear firft made gods, a truth to heathens
    known;
But goddeffes are made by love alone.

But goddefs is a title ftill too mean
For fweet Sophia, pleafure's honour'd queen,
My lovely fair one, youthful, gay, and free,
Shall ne'er affume this falfe divinity,
But leave to city dames fuch proud idolatry.
To her thy temple, harmony, is giv'n,
A nobler palace, and a fairer heav'n,
Whether in Pfyche's form, whilft light'nings
    play,
And thunders roar, fhe joins the plaintive
    lay;
Or whilft the real flame her hearers prove,
Points the keen pangs of difappointed love.

Say,

Say, sweet enchantress, by what pow'r un-
    known
Can'st thou with matchless skill unite in one
The wit of smart Thalia's flippant tongue,
And Polyhymnia's elegance of song?
O how I love thee when thy sportive vein,
Ev'n whilst it mocks, diverts the lover's
    pain!
Whilst, pleasure's little priestess as thou art,
Thy lively sallies captivate the heart.
Never in thy delightful train is seen
The surly pedant, with affected mien
And solemn face, impenetrably dull,
Nor the proud mincing fashionable fool;
Nor in the weaker sex wilt thou permit
Imposing airs to pass for sterling wit;
Nor lov'st thou those proud dames, who think
    it brave
To treat alike the lover and the slave.
Nature we find with thee, or that alone
Which rivals her, the art of fair Ninon;
That art which he who sees through still
    believes,
Which without fraud agreeably deceives;
                        With

With thee we trifle, fport, and laugh, and
    play;
With thee we chat the chearful hours away.
Conftraint, the bane of blifs, is never feen.
To enter there, nor hyp, nor fickly fpleen.
There, free from noife and tumult, is the
    feat
Of private happinefs, the dear retreat
Of gentle peace and foft fecurity,
Where by the public's perfecuting eye
No longer feen, beneath the tented fhade,
Around us all the loves and graces play'd,
Whilft to the more than gods, of lib'ral foul,
Our beauteous Hebe pour'd the nectar'd
    bowl.
There lounging liberty, her elbows plac'd
On the free table, in her arms embrac'd
Two nymphs divine, which ev'ry blifs im-
    prove,
Sweet-fmiling pleafure, and all-healing love.

What are thy titles, glory! what, O fame!
Are all thy honours but an empty name!
This fweet delirium, this enchanting hour
In life's fhort day, is more than wealth or pow'r.
                        Live.

Live then, Sophia, eafy, free, and gay,
Nor caft thy dear-lov'd liberty away.
Henceforth, my charmer, take the wifer part,
Let all partake, but none enflave thy heart.
Thy love wou'd fix one happier than the reft ;
But thy indiff'rence makes a thoufand bleft.

LET.

LETTER VII.

To Mr. PALISSOT, Author of a Comedy called the PHILOSOPHERS.

I RETURN you thanks, Sir, both for your letter and for your performance. Be fo kind as to prepare yourfelf for a long anfwer : old men love to prate a little. In the firft place I muft tell you, I think your piece is extremely well written. The philofopher Crifpinus, walking on all fours, muft have raifed a good laugh, and I make no doubt but my friend * John James will be the firft to join in it. It is an innocent jeft, and has no malice in it. Befides that the citizen of Geneva, being certainly guilty of *læfa comedia*, it was natural for comedy to return the compliment.

It is a very different thing with the citizens of Paris, whom you have brought on the ftage ; that is to be fure not a laughing

---

* The celebrated Jean Jaques Roufféau, of Geneva.

matter.

matter. I can eafily conceive that one fhould
endeavour to ridicule thofe who would ridicule us. Self-defence is always juftifiable;
and I know, with regard to myfelf, if I was
not fo old, I would have a fcuffle with
Meff. Freron and de Pompignan, the former
for vilifying and abufing me five or fix years
together, as I am told by thofe who read
fuch trafh; the latter for having pointed me
out before the whole academy as an old
dotard, who has ftuffed his hiftory with falfe
anecdotes. I was ftrongly tempted to mor-
tify him by a full juftification, and convince
him, that the ftory of the iron mafk, the
teftament of Charles II. of Spain, and feveral others of the fame kind, are abfolutely
true; and that when I mean to be ferious,
I have done with poetical fictions.

I have the vanity to think myfelf worthy
of a place amidft the crowd of Philofophers,
who are always confpiring againft the ftate,
and who moft certainly are the caufe of all
the misfortunes that happen to us by fea and
land. For, to confefs the truth, I was the firft
who

who wrote in France in favour of attraction, againſt the great vortices of Deſcartes, and the little ones of Malebranche. I defy the moſt ignorant wretch, even Freron himſelf, to prove that I have ever falſified the New-tonian ſyſtem. The ſociety at London ap-prove my little catechiſm of attraction; moſt undoubtedly, therefore, I muſt be deemed guilty of philoſophy.

If I had vanity, I ſhould think myſelf ſtill more criminal, according to the report of a certain large book, intitled, *The Oracle of Philoſophers,* which has reached even as far as my retreat. This oracle, may it pleaſe you, is no other than myſelf. I ſhould have burſt with vain-glory, but unhappily my vanity was taken down, when I found that the author of this ſame oracle had pre-tended frequently to have ſeen and dined with me, at a ſeat near Lauſanne, which I never ſet eyes on. He tells you, that I re-ceived him very well, and, in return for this kind reception, he acquaints the public
with

with all the fecrets I had intrufted him
with.

I told him, it feems, that I had been with
the king of Pruffia, on purpofe to eftablifh
the Chinefe religion there. Thus you fee I am
become at once one of the feƈt of Confucius,
and have therefore a right to refent all affronts put upon philofophers. I acknowledged, at the fame time, to this author,
that the king of Pruffia had difcarded me;
a circumftance very poffible, but very falfe,
and concerning which this gentleman has
told a downright lye.

I affured him likewife, it feems, that I had
no attachment to France, at a time when the
king is perpetually heaping favours on me,
continues to me the place of his gentleman
in ordinary, and obliges me by annexing the
moft valuable privileges to my eftate. All
this I frankly acknowledged to this worthy
perfon, only that I might be ranked amongft
the philofophers.

I have

I have moreover dipped into the infernal cabal of the Encyclopœdia. There are at leaſt a dozen articles of mine publiſhed in the three firſt volumes, and had prepared for the ſucceeding part a dozen more, which would have overturned all the orders in the ſtate.

I am withal one of the firſt who made uſe of that vile word *humanity*, againſt which you have made ſo brave an attack in your pretended comedy; after this, to re-fuſe me the name of a philoſopher, would certainly be the moſt crying injuſtice.

So much for myſelf. As to the perſons whom you have attacked in this work, if they have injured you, you have certainly a right to retaliate. It has always been deemed lawful in ſociety to turn into ridicule thoſe who have at any time done us the ſame little favour. I remember, when I lived in the world, I was ſcarce ever preſent at an entertainment, where ſome laugher did not exerciſe his raillery on one

E   of

of the company; who, in his turn, endeavoured to raife the laugh againft his competitor.
Lawyers do the fame at the bar ; and all the
writers I know ridicule one another as much
as they poffibly can. Boileau laughed at
Fontenelle, and Fontenelle at Boileau. The
firft Rouffeau made a jeft of Zara and Al-
zira, and I did the fame by his latter epiftles ;
acknowledging at the fame time, that his
ode on Conquerors was excellent, and moft
of his epigrams very clever ; for above all
things we muft remember to be juft.

Examine your confcience, and fee if you
are fo in reprefenting D'Alembert, Diderot, Helvetius, Jaucourt, and the reft of
them as fo many fcoundrels and pick-
pockets. Again I fay, if they laughed at
you in their books, you have a right to
laugh at them again ; but, by heaven, your
raillery is too ftrong; if they really were fuch
as you have made them, they ought to be
fent to the gallies, which is by no means a
comic fcene. To fpeak plainly to you, thofe
whom you endeavour to reflect on are known

to

to be fome of the beft men in the world;
and I am not certain whether their honour
and integrity are not even fuperior to their
philofophy.

I frankly avow to you I do not know a
more refpectable character than Helvetius,
who has given up two hundred and fifty
thoufand livres a year for the advantage of
cultivating the Belles-Lettres in peace and
quiet. If he has, perhaps, in a large volume,
full of new and fublime things, advanced, by
chance, half a dozen rafh and ill-founding
propofitions, he has already fufficiently re-
pented of them, without having his wounds
torn open by you on a public ftage.

Mr. Duclos, fecretary to the firft academy
in the kingdom, had certainly a title to more
regard than you have fhewn him. His book
on Manners is by no means a bad one. It
is the performance of an honeft man, who
paints ftrongly what he has himfelf feen and
well obferved. In a word, have thefe gentlemen publicly offended you ? It does not

ap-

appear to me that they have. Why then calumniate them fo outragioufly?

I am a ftranger to Mr. Diderot, nor did I ever fee him; I only know he has been unfortunate, and unjuftly perfecuted by fome ignorant and cruel tyrants. This confideration alone fhould have made you drop the pen. I regard withal the defign of the Encyclopœdia, as one of the fineft monuments we could raife to the arts and fciences. There are in it fome excellent articles, not only by D'Alembert, Diderot, and Jaucourt; but by feveral others, who, without any motive of profit or ambition, took a pleaufure in contributing towards that immortal work. There are indeed fome parts of it throughly contemptible, and mine perhaps may be of the number; but there is fo much more of the good than of the bad, that all Europe defires a continuation of the Encyclopœdia. The firft volumes have already been tranflated into feveral languages. Why then expofe and ridicule on the ftage, a work become necef-

fary

fary to the inſtruction of mankind, and the glory of our nation ?

I muſt own to you I am aſtoniſhed at what you tell me concerning Mr. Diderot. He has publiſhed, you aſſure me, two libels againſt two ladies of the firſt rank, who patronize you. You ſaw his name to them in his own hand-writing. If it be really ſo, I have no more to ſay. I deſcend from the clouds, renounce philoſophy, and philoſophers, bid adieu to books, and ſhall think of nothing for the future but my plough and feed-bag. But you will give me leave to aſk you, which I may with juſtice demand, ſome certain proof of this. Permit me to write to theſe ladies friends ; I ſhould be glad to know for certain whether I muſt abſolutely burn my library. But if Mr. Diderot was really wicked enough to abuſe two reſpectable ladies, and what is more, two fine women, did they order you to revenge their cauſe ? And the other characters whom you bring upon the ſtage, have they been ſo rude as to affront theſe ladies alſo ?

Though

Though I never faw Mr. Diderot, I have always had the greateft refpect for his profound knowledge. Not that I find any thing very pleafant in his Father of a Family; yet, prefixed to this piece, there is an epiftle to the princefs of Naffau, which appeared to me as the mafter-piece of eloquence, and the triumph of humanity. Forgive me the expreffion. Twenty people of the beft characters have affured me, he has a good and noble heart. I fhould be forry to be undeceived, though I would gladly know the truth.

Such is the weaknefs of our nature, moft we wifh to learn, what we moft dread to know. I have given you my opinion with the utmoft freedom. If you find in the bottom of your own heart that I am right, obferve what you have to do. If I am in the wrong, tell me fo; make me acknowledge it, and correct me. I aver to you I have no connections with any perfons concerned in the Encyclopœdia, except perhaps Mr. D'Alembert, who writes me a Lacedæmonian letter once in three months. I have indeed for

him

him the greateſt regard, and ſincerely hope
he never was wanting in reſpeĉt to your noble patroneſſes. Once more I beg your per--
miſſion to conſult Mr. —— about this whole
affair.

I have the honour, Sir, to be, with the
trueſt eſteem of your abilities, and the
ſtrongeſt deſire of that peace which * Meſſ.

* The French editor of theſe letters tells us, in
a note on this paſſage, that Paliſſot was remarkable for abuſing and calumniating his beſt friends
and benefaĉtors: that Mr. Helvetius, when he
was in great diſtreſs ſeven years ago, lent him a
hundred louis-d'ors : that he made ſongs upon
Freron and his wife, who ſupported him for four
years : and that, in return for their good offices,
he made the following madrigal, which has
ſome archneſs in it, and which therefore I ſhall
give the reader in the original, together with a
tranſlation of it:

I.

Freron à l'an literaire
Met ſon nom & fait fort bien,
Car il paye ce qu'il fait faire;
Mais des enfans d'un tel pere,
Si chacun reprenoit le ſien,
Monſieur Freron n'auroit plus rien.

II

Freron, Pompignan, and some other bad
writers would fain deprive me of. Your most
obedient, &c. &c.

II.

C'est donc à tort qu'on le blame
D'etre mordant comme un chien,
Il peut faire une epigramme ;
Mais, demandez le à sa femme,
Si chacun reprenoit le sien,
Monsieur Freron n'auroit plus rien.

III.

Il est logé comme un prince,
Mais il doit, je ne scai combien,
J'ai bien peur qu'on ne le pince.
Car son credit est si mince,
Que si chacun reprend le sien,
Monsieur Freron n'aura plus rien.

IV.

Aussi malgré l'étalage
De ses talens & de son bien,
Et de son noble compérage
Tant enfans, meubles, qu'ouvrages,
Quand chacun reprendra le sien,
Monsieur Freron n'aura plus rien.

I. Fre-

I.

Freron, a candidate for fame,
To his *review* has put his name;
And well he might, for he, you'll fay,
May thofe who do it for him pay,
The children for their father writ;
But from this mingled mafs of wit,
Were ev'ry one to take his own,
What would be left for poor Freron ?

II.

'Tis wrong to tax him with ill-nature,
Freron's a poor but harmlefs creature;
Tho', to preferve a poet's name,
He boafts of many an epigram;
Yet fhould you afk the poet's wife,
She would confefs, I'll lay my life,
Were ev'ry one to take his own,
Few would be left for poor Freron.

III.

Lodg'd like a monarch, he forgets,
Like other kings, to pay his debts;
His creditors, a numerous train,
Who threaten hard, his pockets drain,
And fcarce the needy bard, I fear,
Can hold it out another year;
Were ev'ry one to take his own,
What would be left for poor Freron ?

IV;

IV.

Spite of this pompous long parade
Of genius, and of fortune made,
His wealth, his family, and birth,
His wit, his humour, and his worth,
With all the offspring you can find,
Or of his body, or his mind,
Were ev'ry one to take his own,
What would be left for poor Freron?

LET-

LETTER VIII.

To Mr. PALISSOT.

S I R,   Chateau de Ferney, 28 June, 1760.

I AM very angry with you. My refolution was to laugh at every thing in my peaceable retreat; but you have made me melancholy. You load me with praifes, compliments, and friendfhip. I blufh like an Agnes, when you tell the world that I am fuperior to all thofe whom you have attacked.

I believe I can write better verfes than them, and perhaps know as much of hiftory as they do; but, by my God, and upon my foul, (as the Englifh fay) old as I am, I am but a fchool-boy to them in every other refpect. But proceed we to fomething of more confequence.

A friend of mine, of irreproachable character, and worthy of all attention, has affured

fured me, and indeed proved in his laft letter, that Mr. Diderot is not guilty of the
facts which you lay to his charge. Another perfon, no lefs refpectable, has fent me
a long detail of that whole affair, from
whence it plainly appears, that Diderot had
no concern in thofe infamous letters imputed to him. I have never feen, nor
know any thing of him, any more than
that he is engaged with the worthy and
learned D'Alembert in a work which I read
every day with frefh pleafure ; a work, befides, of no lefs than fix hundred thoufand
crowns value in a library, which has already
been tranflated into three or four languages, and yet

Quefta rabbia della gelofia

was quickly armed againft a work, which
would have been an honour to our nation,
and towards which above fifty perfons of
the firft diftinction were eager to contri-
bute ; but one Abraham Chaumeix took it
into his head to write a paper againft the
Encyclopœdia, where he makes the authors
fay

fay what they never meant to fay, and even
argues againſt what they may fay hereafter.
He miſquotes the fathers of the church, as
well as the authors of the dictionary. Abraham Chaumiex notwithſtanding is believed,
the licence withdrawn from the bookſellers,
and procefs iſſued out againſt the authors,
and I, amongſt others, am pointed out in
the indictment, penned by the eloquent and
ſublime Robin, that great benefactor to, and
glory of his age; the eagle of magiſtrates,
and the phœnix of France. Whilſt things
are in this diſagreeable ſituation you write a
comedy againſt the philoſophers, and wound
them when they are *ſub gladio*. The part,
no doubt, of a Chriſtian full of humanity and
charity.

You tell me, in excuſe, that Moliere
laughed at Cotin and Menage. It may be ſo;
but he never aſſerted that Cotin and Menage
advanced immoral tenets; whilſt you attribute to theſe gentlemen the moſt dreadful
maxims, both in your play and the preface
to it.

You

You affure me that you never accufed
Mr. Jaucourt, who notwithftanding is moft
certainly the author of the article GOVERN-
MENT, there is his name in great letters
immediately under it ; you have extracted feveral paffages from it, which may do him
great injury, detached from what goes before, and what follows them, and yet, if
taken all together, are worthy of Tully,
Grotius, or de Thou. You feem befides not
to know that Mr. Jaucourt is of a very illuftrious family, and no lefs refpectable for his
character than for his birth and fortune.

You find fault with a paffage in Mr.
D'Alembert's excellent preface to this work.
Whilft not a word of any fuch paffage is to
be found in it, and impute to Mr. Diderot
what is to be met with only in the Jewifh
letters. Certainly fome Abraham Chaumiex muft have furnifhed you with this
paffage, as he did the Orator of juftice : but
you have done more ; you have added to
your accufations of fome of the worthieft
men in the world, fome fhocking things,
taken

taken from a foolifh pamphlet, called *The Happy Life, or Man a Plant*, which a filly fellow, one La Mettrie wrote in a drunken fit at Berlin, above fifteen years ago. This fatire of La Mettrie, long fince forgotten, and revived by you, has no more relation to philofophy and the Encyclopœdia than the porter of the Chartreux by mafter Gervaife has to the hiftory of the church; and yet you join all thefe accufations together : and what is the confequence ? Your information falls perhaps into the hands of a prince, a minifter, or a magiftrate, bufied in affairs of importance; perhaps of the queen her-felf, ftill more bufy in relieving the indigent, and doing good, and who withal is too much taken up with the neceflary forms attendant on her high ftation to have much leifure. One may have time to read curforily over your preface, which contains but a fheet, and yet not have time to examine and con-front with it that immenfe work to which you impute fuch abominable tenets. No body knows who this La Mettrie is; many perhaps believe he is one of the writers in the

the Encyclopœdia, whom you attack. Thus the innocent, now living, may suffer for the guilty, who are no more. You have done, therefore, more mischief than you thought of, and more than you ever intended; and certainly, if you reflect coolly upon it, must one day feel the most frequent and bitter remorse for it. ˙

Shall I then tell you my sentiments with freedom ? Your comedy has been played, and has succeeded. You have now another kind of glory to acquire, and the only way you can do it is, to make in all the journals a public declaration, carefully drawn up, wherein you should acknowledge, that not having a copy of the Encyclopœdia in your own possession, you had been misled by some unfaithful extracts which had been given you; that you were, as you very reasonably might be, alarmed at such pernicious tenets ; but that having since carefully consulted those passages in which such maxims were supposed to be contained ; having read with attention the preface to that work, and several

other

other articles equally worthy of admiration,
you esteem it a pleasure, as well as duty, to
do all deserved justice to the immense labour
of the authors, the sublime morality spread
throughout their works, and the purity of their
manners. This procedure would not, in my
opinion, be considered as a retractation, which
is the business of those who had misinformed
you. It would, I think, do you a great
deal of honour, and put a happy end to a very
unfortunate quarrel.

This, Sir, is my advice; good or bad I
know not; after which, I will never in any
sort trouble myself with the affair; it has
given me uneasiness, and I would fain spend
the rest of my life in peace and happiness. I
love to laugh. I am old and sickly, and hold
gaiety to be a better remedy even than the
prescriptions of my dear and honoured friend
Tronchin. I shall laugh as much as I can
at those who have laughed at me. This will
divert me, and can do me no harm. A
Frenchman who can't be gay, is out of his
element. You are a writer of comedies; be
joyous

joyous therefore, and do not make the stage
a criminal amusement, that may involve you
in difficulties, and perhaps ruin you. You
are now at your ease ; have a respect for your
masters and protectors. Fortune is blind ;
keep her favours, if you can, by honest means,
and be happy amongst your worthy friends,
if you have *any* such in your cotterie *.

* Chaumeix, the writer mentioned in the above
letter, was formerly under-master in a school.
His principal, a great Jansenist and caballer,
brought him up, and made a convulsionist of him.
This wretch, after having practised several sorts
of trades at Paris, driven from every place, at
last has taken refuge at Petersburgh, where he is
now starving, in the infamous profession of a pa-
rasite, to which he is intirely devoted.

Palissot, so universally known and despised,
did not venture to appear at Paris for a long
time, being obliged by his creditors to leave that
stage of fortune, where knaves play so many capital parts ; at length some people of fashion, to
whose pleasures this satirical poet had been subservient, found themselves under the necessity
of protecting him, and gave him an opportunity
of paying his debts. Rascals are sure of meeting
with encouragement from the great. He soon
shewed his whole character. He was caressed
and employed. By attending to the means of
raising

raifing his fortune, he was in a capacity of acquit-
ting himfelf to his patrons; but, in fpite of all
the favours he received, was forced at laft to
hide himfelf in one of the provinces on the publication of the Dunciad, a work equally contemptible and malicious. This was the only
means he could poffibly take to avoid a beating,
which he would moft certainly have received.
That which he experienced for his comedy of
the Philofophers taught him, that a relapfe in
thefe cafes is generally fatal.

N. B. Thefe two notes are by the French editor
of the letters.

LETTER IX.

To Mr. de la HARPE, Author of the Earl of Warwick, a Tragedy, which was well received.

SIR,   Nov. 1763.

NEXT to the pleafure of reading your excellent tragedy, was that which I received from the letter you did me the honour to write on that occafion. Your principles are good, and your piece confirms them.

Racine, the firft writer amongft us who had tafte, like Corneille, was the firft who had genius alfo. The admirable Racine, never fufficiently admired, thought as you do. The pomp of fpectacle is never a beauty but when it makes a neceffary part of the fubject, otherwife it is no more than decoration. Incidents have no merit but when they are natural, and declamation is always childifh, efpecially when it is ftuffed with bombaft.
            You

You applaud yourfelf for never writing verfes that are to be got by heart, and I, Sir, have found out that you make a great many fuch. The verfes which I get by heart with the greateft eafe, are thofe where the maxim is turned into fentiment, where the poet feems lefs ambitious of appearing himfelf than of fhewing his characters, where no opportunities are fought after to elevate and furprize; where nature alone fpeaks, and nothing is faid but what ought to be faid. Thefe are the verfes which I like; judge if I have not reafon to be fond of yours.

You have a great deal of merit, and therefore muft expect a great many enemies. Formerly, when a man had written any thing good, fomebody told brother Vadeblé that he was a Janfenift, brother Vadeblé told it to father Tellier the Jefuit, who told it to the king; at prefent, if you write a good tragedy, they will fay you are an atheift. It is pleafant enough to hear the abufe which the * abbé d'Aubignac, the king's preacher, has

* D'Aubignac, fays the French editor, in a note on this paffage, a bad preacher, and a ftill
z   worfe

lavished on the author of *Cinna*. At all times there have been * Frerons in literature; but they say, one must have gnats for nightingales to devour, that they may sing the better.

worse writer and poet, published two volumes on the theatre, which are detestable. He was an enemy of the great Corneille, and abused him frequently in the grossest manner.

D'Aubignac's *Pratique du Theatre*, or Practice of the Stage, is notwithstanding, with all due deference both to Mr. Voltaire and his editor, a very good book, and contains many useful observations on the conduct of the drama.

* Mr. de la Harpe was abused by Freron, and nick-named by him the Baby of the Stage, after the name of the king of Poland's dwarf. De la Harpe, to be revenged on this hangman of Parnassus, wrote the following tolerable epigram:

Bufo, prepar'd to bid the world good night,
Sends for his priest to set all matters right;
Struck with remorse, he makes a long confession
Of many a heinous vice, and foul transgression,
Whoring and drinking, base hypocrisy,
Impudence, lying, and malignity.
And is this all, cries Dominic? Run o'er
The rest, my friend.—Indeed I have no more.
You have forgot, reply'd the priest, by chance,
One crying sin—the sin of—ignorance.

LETTER X.

To Mr. * B L I N, Author of the heroic
Epiftles of GABRIELLE D'ESTREES,
miftrefs of Henry IV.

Ferney, Feb. 1762.

THANKS to my friend—when men like
you admire,
It fooths our pride, and fans the poet's fire.
Never was love in fweeter fong difplay'd;
Never was truth with finer art betray'd.
Critics, perhaps, the taftelefs world may tell
Your dying Gabrielle only talks too well; ·

* Mr. Blin, as the French editor of thefe letters informs us, is author of feveral heroic epiftles,
and other pieces of poetry univerfally admired.
His ftile is eafy, and his manner agreeable. He
exerted himfelf with great warmth and humanity
in the affair of Calas, which was reheard by the
chamber of requefts, compofed of forty-five fenfible and upright judges, who gained immortal
honour by their decifion of it.   There are feveral
good copies of verfes of Mr. Blin's in the collection of poems in three volumes, 12mo. publifhed by Mr. Lunan de Boifgermain.

But

But feeling hearts compaſſionate her pains,
Pity her paſſion, and applaud her ſtrains.
She look'd for pardon to offended heav'n,
And hop'd a fault like hers might be forgiv'n.
And ſo it might, for 'twas a pious thing
To love ſo dearly our moſt-chriſtian king.
Such fond and tender hearts- ev'n ſaints
  approve ;
The damn'd are thoſe alone who nothing
  love.

LET-

LETTER XI.

Suppofed to be written by Father CHARLES GOUJU to his Brethren the Jefuits.

I Conjure, not you only, my dear fellow-countrymen, but all my dear brethren of Germany, Italy, and England, to reflect ferioufly with me, for your edification, on what is at prefent going forward with regard to our right reverend fathers the Jefuits, both the well-doing and the well-faying.

I am coufin to Mr. Cazot, and related to Mr. Lionci, whom the right reverend father la Valette, the apoftolical firft lord of trade, has totally demolifhed. The lord will, no doubt, have mercy on his firft director; but I would beg leave to afk any man who makes ufe of his reafon, whether it is pof-fible that father la Valette, after ftudying theology for two years, had really any belief in the Chriftian religion, when, after making a folemn vow of poverty, and con-

F   fulting

fulting the gofpel, he traded for fix millions? Is there the leaft probability in nature, that a grave divine, of fo much faith and piety, fhould, with fo much eafe and indifference, run the hazard of his falvation, by doing any thing fo inconfiftent with his vows, and fo directly oppofite to his religion?

That one of the faithful, mifled by the violence of his paffions, fhould for once be guilty of a crime, and repent of it, might be expected from the frailty of our nature; but when the mafters in Ifrael rob and plunder, whilft they are preaching and fhriving; when they exercife themfelves in this manner for whole years together, I muft afk you, my dear brethren, if you think it poffible that they fhould thus be always perfuaded themfelves, and always deceiving others? That they fhould think of carrying God in their hands at mafs, and pillage their neighbours as foon as they come from the holy table?

It

It appears from the depofitions of the con-
fpirators at Lifbon, that their confeffors the
Jefuits had affured them, they might fafely,
and with a good confcience, affaffinate the
king. I would only beg to know whether
thofe who made ufe of a facrament to excite
men to a parricide, could really believe in
that facrament ?

But to pafs from thefe enormous crimes to
iniquities of another kind. Do you imagine
that the Jefuit Tellier believed in Jefus Chrift?
Do you even fuppofe he could believe in a juft
God, the rewarder of good and evil, whilft
he abufed the ignorance of Lewis XIV. in
religious matters, on purpofe to perfecute
the virtuous cardinal de Noailles, when making no fcruple to commit forgery, he fhewed
his penitentiary letters from feveral bifhop's
which thofe bifhops had never written ?
Does not this conduct, perfevered in for feveral years, fufficiently demonftrate that the
confeffor did not himfelf believe a word of
what he taught?

The

The adverfaries of the Jefuits likewife, who pretended to convulfions and fo many other miracles, and who have been convicted of fo many impoftures, were they better believers than father Tellier?

I fay again, a man may believe in God, and yet kill his father; but is it poffible he fhould believe in God, and pafs his whole life amidft deliberate crimes, and an uninterrupted feries of fraud and impofture? He muft repent at laft, in his laft moments; but I defy you to find in hiftory one fingle divine who ever acknowledged his crimes on his death-bed.

Amongft the laity we frequently fee men, who have been guilty of inceft and murder, making public acknowledgement of their fins; but I will be bound to forfeit ten thoufand crowns, the remains of all that fortune which father la Valette robbed me of, if you can produce me one penitent divine.

Shall I give you fome ftill more noble examples? Take them from your firft popes.

Julius

Julius II. with his helmet and coat of armour, the voluptuous Leo X. Alexander VI. polluted with incests and assassinations, so many sovereign pontiffs surrounded by mistresses and bastards, laughing at the credulity of mankind in the bosom of riot and debauchery, think you that these ever lifted up to God hands filled with gold, or stained with blood ? Did one of them ever repent in their retirement ? Whilst we behold Charles the fifth chaunting his *de profundis* to every saint in the Calendar. In every age the true unbelievers, great or little, shaved or mitred, have been all, divines.

If I am not mistaken, this is the manner in which they all argued. The Christian religion which I teach is most certainly not that of the primitive times. It is clear that the communion of the first Christians was not a private mass ; it is equally indisputable that the images we invoke were forbidden for more than the two first centuries; that auricular confession was for a long time utterly unknown; that all our rites have

been

been changed, not excepting one of them, and our tenets alfo. We know when the addition was made to the fymbol of the apoftles, touching the procedure of the Holy Spirit. Amongft all thofe opinions, which have coft fo much bloodfhed, there is not one which can be fairly deduced from the gofpel; all is our own work, and all arbitrary: we cannot poffibly therefore believe what we teach; we have nothing to do then but to avail ourfelves of the folly of mankind; we may venture, without fear, to fhrive our neighbours, and plunder them; to affaffinate them, and give them extreme unction.

It is apparent not only that they muft have argued thus, but that it is impoffible they fhould have argued in any other manner; for once more I affirm, it is not in nature for a man to fay, I firmly believe what I teach, and yet act the direct contrary during my whole life, and even at the laft moment of it.

The laity, indeed, efpecially among the great, have imitated the clergy in all religions. Muftapha faid, my mufti does not

believe

believe in Mahomet, I ought not therefore to believe in him myfelf, and may ftrangle my brothers without any fear or fcruple whatfoever.

That abominable fyllogifm, *my religion is falfe, therefore there is no God*, is as common as any thing I know, and the moft fertile fource of every crime.

What, my brethren, becaufe Malagrida is an Affaffin, le Tellier a forger, la Valette a bankrupt, and the mufti a knave, muft it follow that there is no fupreme being, no creator and preferver, no equitable judge, to punifh or reward? I knew a Jacobin friar, a doctor of the Sorbonne, who turned atheift, becaufe the prior of his convent obliged him to maintain within the walls of his cloyfter that the virgin Mary was born in fin, whilft in the Sorbonne he was forced to fupport the contrary. This man faid very coolly, my religion is falfe: if my religion, therefore, which is beyond all difpute the beft in the world, carries with it the marks of falfhood, there can be no fuch thing as religion, nor

any

any fuch thing as a God. What a fool was I
to become a Jacobin at the age of fifteen !

I had compaffion on this poor man, and
talked to him : My dear friend, faid I, you
were certainly a great fool for becoming a
Jacobin ; but whether the virgin Mary was
maculate or immaculate, would God therefore lofe his exiftence ? Would he be lefs the
judge and father of mankind ? Does he not
command the firft Colar of China, as well as
the loweft Jacobin, to be juft, temperate,
and fincere, and do unto every one as he
would wifh fhould be done unto him, and
to love one another in honour ? Tenets
change, my friend ; but God never changeth.
The Cordelier St. Bonaventure, and the Ja-.
cobin St. Thomas, are fcarce ever of the
fame opinion ; neverthelefs they are, with a
number of other faints, encircling the throne
of glory, and waiting for many more who
reafon no better than themfelves. Never do
you think like Thomas, or like Bonaventure. Some books have been mifinterpreted,
others forged ; does that give you concern ?

Comfort

Comfort yourſelf, my friend ; the great volume of nature cannot be miſinterpreted :
there it is written, Adore one God ; be juſt
and charitable, kind and benevolent. If the
holy fathers, the children of Ignatius, had
given this excellent precept a place in their
Catholic Catechiſm, they might have filled
the world with good and valuable men : they
might have ranked with other ſaints in the
circle of God, and we ſhould not, as we now
do, have congratulated mankind on their deſtruction.

I perceived, on concluding, that my ſermon, though a little too long, had made a
ſtrong impreſſion on my * Jacobin.

* Father la Valette, ſo well known amongſt
us, was three years at London after the famous
bankruptcy of his ſociety. He went by the name
of le chevalier Duclos, and aſſumed the character
of a † financier in that large city, the general re-

† This is an excellent and ſenſible letter.—How little
ſhould we have to complain of with regard to this ingenious
writer's re.igious opinions,

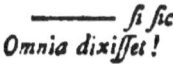

fort

fort of foreign adventurers. He feemed to be of opinion, that having cheated the fociety of Jefus, he might alfo take the liberty to cheat fome of his particular friends. He left London very fuddenly about fifty thoufand crowns in debt, to play fome new part on another ftage. This fharper was feen afterwards at Liege, and decamping from thence, now wanders about, levying contributions in every place on all fuch fools as judge of men only by external appearance.

N. B. This note is fubjoined by the French editor. It is not eafy to determine what he means by the word Financier in this place, as we have no Englifh word properly correfpondent to it, except perhaps that of an excifeman, an office which would hardly have been entrufted to this gentleman. I am rather inclined to think he meant a kind of private banker, broker, or dealer in money-matters, probably only amongft thofe of his own perfuafion. This whole ftory of his refidence in London feems to want confirmation.

LETTER XII.

To Mr. D'ALEMBERT.

THOUGH fome pedants among us have warmly attacked philofophy, they have had no great reafon to value themfelves upon it, as fhe can now boaft of her alliance with the northern powers. The emprefs of Ruffia's excellent letter has given you ample revenge. It puts us in mind of the epiftle which Philip wróte to Ariftotle, with this difference only, that Ariftotle accepted the honourable employment, the education of Alexander, which you have the glory of refufing.

I remember, when I was young, I had no Idea that the time would ever come when fuch a letter fhould be written from Mofcow to a member of the French academy. I was an eye-witnefs of the rife of that empire, and behold! four women have

at

at length completed what one man had be-
gun.

Surely fome compliments are due from our
native gallantry to the fair fex, on a circumftance fo extraordinary, and of which hiftory
can furnifh us with no example. What a
charming letter has this Catherine wro:e!
Neither St. Catherine of Boulogne, nor St.
Catherine of Sienna ever wrote half fo good a
one. If princeffes apply themfelves to the
cultivation of their minds, the Salic law
muft quickly be abolifhed.

Have you not obferved, my dear friend,
that all our great examples, and all our moft
ufeful knowledge, comes from the north?
Newton, Locke, Guftavus, Peter, and the
reft of them, were not educated at Rome, in
the college *de Propaganda.*

I have read lately a moft voluminous * apology for the Jefuits, wherein all the great ge-

---

* This apology for the Jefuits was written by
father Ceruti, at prefent an abbé. This man,
who

niufes of our age are enumerated.—They are all Jefuits. There is, fays the author, Pe-ruffau, Neuville, Griffet, Chapelain, Bau-dori, Buffier, Debillon, Caftel, Laborde, Briet, Garnier, Pezenas, Siennez, Hut, and

who was formerly a Jefuit, is patronifed by the princefs of Carignan, who has given him an apartment in her own palace at Paris. Some Janfenifts fcruple not alfo to affert, that both the apologift and his brother Berthier have private penfions from feveral ladies about the court, ftrongly attached to the late modeft and humble fociety of Jefuits.

D'Alembert certainly deferves the thanks of his countrymen, for his generous refufal of the offer made him by rhe emprefs of Ruffia. It is noble in a queen to invite a philofopher to her court, to inftruct her fon, and teach him to pro-mote the happinefs and glory of his country; but a Frenchman, whofe merit and virtues are all that he can boaft, fhould never banifh himfelf, but remain devoted to his country, and his friends. Perdition on thofe weak and in-conftant minds, who fell to foreigners their talents and their fervice! A Frenchman fhould not, can-not, indeed, live with any fatisfaction out of his own country. Of this Voltaire is a miferable ex-ample, which fhould be a warning to all men of fenfe and abilities, and teach them to avoid the great, their moft cruel and contemptible enemies. To be happy with thefe, we muft be ambitious,

mean,

to crown all, fays he, the great Berthier, who has fo long been the oracle of men of letters. Now I proteft (and I have as good a right to be believed as Mr. Chicaneau) I never heard of any of thefe gentlemen, except brother Berthier, the journalift, who I thought died on his way to Verfailles, and who unfortunately confeffed himfelf, without knowing it, to the ecclefiaftical gazetteer the abbé Poignard, who refufed him abfolution three times.

I am very glad to find that France can ftill boaft of fo many great men. I am told, that, amongft thefe fublime geniufes, there is one Mr. Le Roi, a famous preacher, whofe eloquence is equal to that of father Garaffe. To fpeak ferioufly, if any thing does honour to the age we live in, it is, in my opinion,

mean, and dirty. The man of merit fhould never fo debafe and proftitute himfelf, as to offer incenfe to fuch idols. They are unworthy the regard of genius, and only fit to be a prey to flatterers and courtezans.

N. B. This note by the French editor.

the

the three memorials of Mariette, Beaumont, and l'Oiſeau, in favour of the unfortunate family of Calas. Thus to employ their time, their eloquence, and their credit, and without any reward, to ſuccour the oppreſſed; this is truly great, and brings us nearer to the times of Cicero and Hortenſius than thoſe of Briet, de Hut, and brother Berthier. I have pleaſing expectations of the judgment that will be given. Thank heaven, Europe has already determined it, and I know of no more infallible tribunal than that of all honeſt men, in different countries, joining in the ſame opinion: they form together a body corporate, which cannot err, becauſe it has not that ſpirit which in other bodies corporate doth generally preſide.

I know nothing of the little libel you mention, where I am abuſed for my Examen of ſome pieces of Crebillon. I am a ſtranger both to the Examen, and the abuſe of it. I ſhould have enough to do, if I were to read all theſe beggarly ſcraps. Peter the Great and Corneille find me ſufficient employment.

I have

I have got as far as Pertharite, and intend to portion out the niece of that noble writer to comfort myfelf under the abufe which I expect for it. We fhall put it into the contract that fhe is coufin-german to Chimene, and that fhe is no relation to Grimauld, or Mulple. Perhaps fhe may have had a child before the edition is finifhed. A number of people of fafhion have fubfcribed generoufly. The graver fays their names are not quite fo valuable as bank-bills.

I have fent the academy my tranflation of Heraclius from Calderon. You will fee which is the original, Calderon or Corneille. You will die with laughing at fome parts of it; you will find, notwithftanding, in Calderon, fome fine ftrokes of genius. You will receive foon my General Hiftory alfo. The picture which I have drawn this time of human nature is a three-quarters length; in the other editions it was only a profile. Old as I am, I begin to know it better every Day.

Adieu,

Adieu, my dear and illuſtrious philoſopher. I am obliged to dictate this; for I grow blind, like la Motte. When the abbé Trublet knows this, perhaps he will have a better opinion of my verſes.

LET-.

LETTER XIII.

To his Royal Highneſs the ELECTOR
PALATINE, at Manheim.

Ferney, Aug. 14. 1761.

WOU'D gracious heaven hear the pray'r,
And grant the wiſh of poor Voltaire,
'Twou'd be to ſee the happy day,
When news moſt welcome ſhall impart
Joy unfeign'd to ev'ry heart,
   And I with honeſt rapture ſay,
* I've ſeen the lovely babe, my fears are o'er,
Theſe aged eyes ſhall wiſh to ſee no more.

Your highneſs will pardon this enthuſiaſm;
my tranſport muſt plead my excuſe. I know
not what I am doing. My letter, I fear, is
wanting in the etiquette. At the birth of the
duke of Burgundy, all the boys danced in the
apartments of Lewis XIV. I ſhould be a

---

* The original is an alluſion to a paſſage of
ſcripture, and borders a little upon the profane.

great

great boy at Schwetzingen, if I could have the happiness of throwing myself at the feet of the father, mother, and child. Peace and an heir together are fortunate events indeed. I fall at your knees, my lord, and embrace them with joy. You and the electrefs will pardon, I hope, my bad profe, my bad verfes, my profound refpect, and the intoxication of my heart, and condefcend to prefefve fome regard for your little Swifs,

VOLTAIRE.

LETTER XIV.

To his Royal Highnefs the ELECTOR
PALATINE, at Manheim.

Ferney, Sept. 9, 1761,

'TIS over then : I give you joy,
My noble friend, or girl or boy,
It matters not; when Providence
Thinks fit her bleffings to difpenfe,
She keeps her fecrets cover'd o'er,
Nor lets us know her mind before :
* And we, poor mortals, good or ill,
Wife, foolifh, great, or little, ftill
Muft blindly her behefts fulfil.

  * The fame thought is to be met with in one
of our beft poets :

———— this coercive force
Without your choice muft take its courfe.
                        Great

As we know nothing of her plan,
Muſt grope our way out as we can.
The machiniſt, you underſtand,
Who is above, with pow'rful hand
Directs the whole; and man, I ween,
Is nothing but a poor machine.
Perhaps all is not as it cou'd be;
But all, no doubt, is as it ſhou'd be.
We know, of all the worlds at leaſt
That cou'd have been, this is the beſt;

Great kings to wars are pointed forth,
As loaded needles to the north;
And thou and I, by pow'r unſeen,
Are barely paſſive, and ſuck'd in
To Heinault's vaults, or Celia's chamber,
As ſtraw and paper are by amber.
If we ſit down to play, or ſet
(Suppoſe at ombre or baſſet)
Let people call us cheats or fools,
Our cards and we are equal tools.
We ſure in vain the cards condemn,
Ourſelves both cut and ſhuffle them.
In vain on fortune's aid rely;
She only is a ſtander-by.
Poor men! poor papers! we and they
Do ſome impulſive force obey,
And are but play'd with—do not play.

And,

And, fpite of ficknefs, grief, and pain,
We have no reafon to complain.

To have a fon and heir, tho' late,
Were doubtlefs better for the ftate;
And if a fon like you is giv'n,
It is the nobleft gift of heav'n.

If haply 'tis a daughter—well,
I greet you; for on her fhall dwell
Each grace and beauty, that unite
To catch the gazing lover's fight,
And draw admirers to her arms,
The rival of her mother's charms.

Illuftrious pair! if ever I,
As poets may, can prophefy,
The offspring of thy nuptial bed,
Or fmiling boy, or beauteous maid,
Shall be the theme of ev'ry tongue,
And worthy them from whom it fprung.

And yet, my lord, in fpite of all I have
faid, the affair is of confequence to me, and
I would come foft immediately to know

which

which it is, if that fame Providence, which
does all for the beft, had not treated me
moft cruelly. She has indeed ufed your
poor little old Swifs extremely ill, and made
me the moft miferable, decrepid, and fhri-
velled mortal which this beft of all poffible
worlds can produce.

I fhould really make an excellent figure
amidft the rejoicings of your electoral highnefs. It was only, I think, in the Egypt of
antiquity that fkeletons were admitted to a
place in their feftivals. To fay the truth,
my lord, it is all over with me. I laugh
indeed fometimes; but am forced to acknowledge that pain is an evil. It is a comfort to me that your highnefs is well; but I
am fitter for an extreme unction than a bap-
tifm. May the peace ferve for an æra to
mark the prince's birth ; and may his * au-

* Mr. Voltaire has praifed with the greateft
degree of juftice this excellent prince and princefs,
who in the eafieft and politeft manner take a
pleafure in diftinguifhing all the men of letters
and genius who frequent their court, which is
re-

guſt father preſerve his regard for, and accept the profound reſpects of, his little
Swiſs,

VOLTAIRE.

remarkable for its taſte, magnificence, and every
virtue which adorns humanity.

LET-

LETTER XV.

To Mr. DIODATI, on his Diſſertation
on the Italian Language.

SIR,   Ferney, Jan. 24, 1761.

I AM thoroughly ſenſible of the honour
you did me, by your kind preſent of a treatiſe on the excellency of the Italian tongue :
it was ſending a lover an eulogium on his miſtreſs. You will notwithſtanding pardon me,
I hope, a few reflections in favour of the
French language. When a miſtreſs palls
upon us, we may ſometimes take the part
of a wife.

No language, I believe, is intirely perfect.
It happens in this, as in many other things,
that the learned receive laws from the ignorant. It is the multitude who have formed
every language : the workmen have given
names to their inſtruments : the people got

G   toge-

together and invented terms to exprefs their feveral wants and neceffities; and, after a number of years, the men of genius who rofe up were obliged to make ufe, as well as they could, of fuch phrafes and expreffions as had been eftablifhed by mere chance, and the caprice of a multitude.

I think there are but two languages in the world that are truly harmonious, the Greek and the Latin. They are indeed the only ones whofe verfe has any true meafure, the certain rythmus, a proper mixture of dactyls and fpondees, and a real value in the fyl-lables. The ignorant people who formed thefe languages had certainly a better tafte, a finer ear, and fenfes more delicate than other nations.

You have indeed, as you obferve, long and fhort fyllables in your beautiful Italian tongue, and fo have we; but neither you nor we, nor any other people have the true dactyl and fpondee. Our verfes are cha-racterifed by the number, and not by the fyllable.

fyllable. *La bella lingua Tofcana,* fay you, *e la figlie primogenita del Latino.* True, Sir, enjoy your birth-right; but let the younger fifters come in for their part of the patrimony.

I have always looked upon the Italians as our mafters; but you muft acknowledge we are good difciples. Almoft every language in Europe has its beauties and its faults. You have not thofe melodious noble terminations of the Spaniards, which a happy union of vowels and confonants renders fo fonorous.; *las Ombres, las Hiftorias, los Cotumbres:* You want likewife the diphthongs, which have fo melodious an effect in our language; *les rois, les empereurs, les exploits, les hiftoires.* You find fault with our *e* mute, which you call a harfh and melancholy found, which expires as it were in the mouth; and yet in the *e* mute principally confifts the great harmony both of our profe and verfe. *empire, cou-*

* The beautiful Italian language is the eldeft daughter of the Latin.

G 2　　　　　　　　　　*ronne,*

ronne, diadéme, flamme, tendreffe, victoire, all these happy terminations leave a found in the ear, after the pronunciation of the word, like a harpfichord, that rings after the finger is off the keys.

You muſt allow that the vaſt variety of these falls muſt have ſome advantage over the five ſingle terminations of every word in your language; and even out of these five you muſt take away the laſt: for you have not above ſeven or eight words that end in *u*; ſo that there are in effect only four founds, *a, e, i, o,* that finiſh every Italian word.

Do you really think the ear of a foreigner can be charmed, when he reads for the firſt time, *il capitano ch'el grand ſepolcro libero di Criſto, e che molto opro col ſenno, et colla mano?* Can you imagine all these founds can be agreeable to an ear unaccuſtomed to them? Compare with this dull dry uniformity, ſo diſagreeable to a foreigner, these two plain verſes of Corneille:

Le

Le destin se declare, & nous venons d'entendre
Ce qu'il a résolu du beau-pere & du gendre.

You may obferve every word has a different termination. Pronounce now thefe two
verfes of Homer:

Εξ ȣ δη τα πρωτα διαςητην εριϲαντι
Ατρειδης τι αναξ ανδρων, κ̓ διος Αχιλλιυς.

Pronounce thefe verfes before any young perfon, Englifh or German, who has any ear,
they will certainly prefer the Greek, barely
fuffer the French, and be fhocked with the
perpetual repetition of the fame termination
in the Italian. This I have myfelf feveral
times experienced.

You boaft the extraordinary copioufnefs of
your language; you will at the fame time
allow we are none of the pooreft. There is
in reality no idiom in the world which ex-
preffes all the gradations of things : they are
all poor in this refpect. None of them, for
example, can exprefs, in one word, that love

G 3   which

which is founded on efteem, or that which is founded on beauty alone; that which arifes from a conformity of manners, and that which fprings from the neceffity of loving fomething. Thus it is with all the paffions and qualities of the foul, that which we feel the moft, is what we moft ftand in need of words to exprefs.

But do not imagine, Sir, we are reduced to the extreme indigence which you reproach us with. You have made out a long catalogue, of two pages, of your fuperfluities, and our poverty. On one fide, you have placed *orgoglio*, *alterigia*, *fuperbia*, and on the other only *orgueil*; but befides *orgueil*, Sir, we have *fuperbe*, *hauteur*, *fierté*, *elevation*, *dedain*, *arrogance*, *infolence*, *gloire*, *gloriole*, *prefomtion*, *outre-cuidance*; all thefe words exprefs the different fhades and gradations of pride, in the fame manner as with you *orgoglio*, *alterigia*, *fuperbia*, are not always fynonimous.

In your alphabet you find fault with us for having but one word to fignify *valiant*. I know

I know very well, Sir, that your nation is very valiant when it has a mind, or other people havé a mind that it ſhould be ſo ; both Germany and France have been ſo happy as to have in their ſervice many brave and noble Italian officers.

L'Italico valor non é ancor morto.

But if you have *valente, prode, animoſo,* we alſo have *vaillant, valeureux, preux, courageux, intrepide, hardi, animé, audacieux, brave,* &c. Courage and bravery have ſeveral different characters, which are expreſſed by ſo many different words. We would ſay our generals are valiant, couragious, brave ; but we would diſtinguiſh the lively and bold courage of that general, who carried ſword in hand all the works at Port-mahon, cut out of the live rock, from that deliberate, conſtant, active firmneſs with which one of our chiefs ſaved a whole garriſon from inevitable deſtruction, and marched thirty leagues in ſight of the enemy's forces, conſiſting of thirty thouſan d.

We

We would exprefs differently alfo that calm intrepidity which fome pretended connoiffeurs admired in the youngeft nephew of the hero of the Valteline, who feeing his army routed, occafioned by the panic of our allies at Rofbach, which produced our own alfo, having obferved the regiment of Diefbach and one more who ftood firm and unbroken, as if they had been victorious, though they were furrounded by the cavalry, and battered by the cannon, marched up to them alone, praifed their valour, firmnefs, intrepidity, patience, boldnefs, fpirit, bravery, &c. You fee, Sir, what a number of terms we have to exprefs one thing. Afterwards he had the courage to rally thefe two regiments, and fave them from an imminent danger, which their extraordinary bravery had led them into, conducted them fafely in the face of a victorious enemy; and fhewed ftill greater ftrength of mind, in fupporting the bitter and inexhauftible reproaches of the foolifh multitude, who are always too foon and too well acquainted with every thing, be it good or bad.

You

You may remark, Sir, that the courage, valour, and firmnefs of the men who guarded Caffel and Gottingen, and held out againft fixty thoufand of the enemy, was a courage compofed of activity,. boldnefs, and fore-fight; as was that alfo of him who faved Wezel. Believe then, Sir, I intreat you, that we have in our language a power of ex-preffing every thing which the defenders of our country have the power to perform.

You infult us alfo with the word *ragout*, as if it were the only term we had to exprefs our feveral courfes. I wifh to God you were right; it would be better, I believe, for my health; but, unhappily for us, we have a whole kitchen dictionary full of them.

You feem proud of having two words that fignify *glutton*; but pray, Sir, call to mind, and at the fame time lament, our *gourmands*, *goulus*, *friands*, *mangeurs*, and *gloutons*.

For the *man of knowledge* you don't remem-ber that we have any word befides *favant*;

G 5   but

but be pleafed, Sir, to add *docte, erudit, in-fruit, eclairé,* you will find, I believe, both the name and the thing amongft us; and thus it is with regard to every thing you have reproached us for. We have indeed no diminutives, though we had as many as you in the time of Marot, Rabelais, and Montaigne; but this puerile mode of expreffion feemed beneath the dignity of a language ennobled by fuch writers as Pafcal, Boffuet, Fenelon, Peliffon, Corneille, Boileau, Racine, Maffillon, Fontaine, la Bruyere, and Rouffeau. We left the *ottes* and *ettes* to Ronfard, Marot, and Dubartas, and only kept *fleurette, amourette, fillette, grandelette, veillotte, nabotte, maifonette,* and *villotte;* and even thefe we never make ufe of when we fpeak or write in the familiar ftile. Don't imitate Matthei therefore, who, in his fpeech to the academy of la Crufca, dwells fo largely on the vaft advantage of calling *corbello corbellino,* forgetting at the fame time that we have *corbeil* and *corbillon.*

You have advantages over us of much greater confequence, that particularly of inverfions

verfions. You can make a hundred good
verfes in Italian with more eafe than we can
make fix in French, and the reafon is, becaufe you allow yourfelves, that *hiatus*, thofe
gapings of fyllables which we don't admit of,
becaufe all your words end in *a, e, i,* or *o,*
becaufe you have at leaft twenty times as
many rhimes as we have, and becaufe, which
is ftill more defirable, you can do without
any rhymes at all.

But do not reproach our language with
roughnefs, bad profody, barrenefs, or obfcurity; your own tranflations* prove the contrary. Read moreover every thing that Meff.
D'Olivet and du Marfais have faid concerning the manner of fpeaking our language

---

* Diodati tranflated into Italian the *Peruvian
Letters,* by M. de Grafiigny, and publifhed them,
in 2 vol. 12mo. with the original. His *Differta-
tion on the Italian Language* was much talked of,
probably on account of the above letter from
Voltaire concerning it. The French editor tells
us, in a note on this letter, that Voltaire only
wrote it to make his court to fome great people,
and give himfelf an air of importance with men
of literature.

with

with propriety. Read Mr. Duclos, and Douchet; obferve with what force and per-fpicuity, with what energy and grace, Mr. D'Alembert and Mr. Diderot exprefs them-felves! what picturefque phrafes are often made ufe of by du Buffon, Helvetius, and Roufſeau, even in works that do not appear fufceptible of them!

I ſhall put an end to this letter, already too long, by one reflection; if to the com-mon people we owe the formation of lan-guages, to great writers we are indebted for the perfection of them; and the beſt of all languages is that which can boaſt of the beſt works in it.

I have the honour to be, with the greateſt efteem, both for yourfelf and the Italian lan-guage,

SIR,

Your, &c. &c.

A N-

ANOTHER ANSWER

FROM

Mr. VOLTAIRE to Mr. DIODATI.

Eerney, Feb. 1, 1761.

I.

TALK not to me of your exalted worth,
Your wealth, your fame, your honours, and
    your birth;
'Tis foolish pride, my friend; you seldom see
Men, highly born, boast of their pedigree.

II.

Tho' France has long by Italy been taught,
And still reveres her mistress as she ought;
                                        Yet

Yet keen reproach, like yours, may pay the
    debt,
And make the warmeſt gratitude—forget.

III.

Beyond our childhood, we have quitted long
Our ancient nurſe, and now are grown ſo
    ſtrong,
We ſcorn the milk which once our weaker
    frame
Suſtain'd, and proud return from whence we
    came.

IV.

If aught could make us jealous, 'twere the
    ſong
† Of Diodati in his rival's tongue.
Do not thy own fair image then deface,
Nor do an inj'ry where thou ow'ſt a grace.

   † Alluding to his elegant tranſlations from
the French.

V.

V.

No longer let us fquabble for the prize,.
Equality, you know, contents the wife:
Henceforth let this thy happinefs enhance,
'Tis no difgraceful lot to rival France..

LETTER XVI.

To Mr. BAILLON, Intendant of Lyons, on account of a poor Jew taken up for uttering contraband Goods.

BLESSINGS on the Old Teſtament, which gives me this opportunity of telling you, that amongſt all thoſe who adore the New, there is not one more devoted to your ſervice than myſelf, a certain deſcendant of Jacob, a pedlar, as all theſe gentlemen are, whilſt he is waiting for the Meſſiah, waits alſo for your protection, which at preſent he has the moſt need of. Some honeſt men, of the firſt trade of St. Matthew, who gather together the Jews and Chriſtians at the gates of your city, have ſeized ſomething in the breeches pocket of an Iſraelitiſh page, belonging to the poor circumciſed, who has the honour to tender you this billet, with all proper ſubmiſſion and humility. I beg leave to join my Amen to his at a venture.

I but

I but juſt ſaw you at Paris as * Moſes ſaw the Deity, and ſhould be very happy in ſeeing you face to face. If the word face can any ways be applied to me, preſerve ſome remembrance of your old eternal humble ſervant, who loves you with that chaſte and tender affection, which the religious Solomon had for his three hundred Shunamites.

* See Voltaire's Dictionaire Philoſophique.

L E T.

LETTER XVII.

To the Count de SERBETTI, on the new Edition of Corneille.

SIR,   Ferney, Aug. 13, 1762.

I AM old, infirm, and overloaded with useless and unneceſſary employments, three excuses for not anſwering your kind letter. I find them all three diſagreeable enough; I bear the weakneſs of my own dotage tolerably; but cannot ſo well reconcile myſelf to that of Corneille, which nevertheleſs muſt, it ſeems, be publiſhed; becauſe the world, who have not ſo much taſte as curioſity, will have all a man's follies, as well as his works. I know you are a lover of truth, and becauſe you think ſhe is dear to me alſo, pardon my poor abilities. I flatter myſelf you will find ſome proofs of my adherence to her in the new edition of my General Hiſtory. I had ſketched human nature; I hope now I have drawn her at full length.

I be—

I believe Meff. Cramer the bookfellers propofe publifhing thefe additions in a fepa-rate volume. I leave the correction of the the prefs intirely to them, as I have no * in-tereft in the affair. All I have to do is to fearch out the truth as well as I can, and the applaufe of men of merit like yourfelf is my reward.

I am, with the greateft refpect,

Your's, &c.

* Mr. Voltaire (fays the French editor) gave away all the profits of his *Univerfal Hiftory* to the bookfellers of Geneva, and has made prefents of all his productions for thefe fifteen years paft, either to actors, or fome of his particular friends. Mr. Voltaire's enemies either do not believe this, or can fee very little merit in it. Such inftances. of generofity are notwithftanding very rare. We fhould praife the meritorious actions of an ene-my, as well as a friend. Any man who, as Vol-taire did, could portion out the niece of the great Corneille, would furely deferve to be immor-talized.

L E T-

LETTER XVIII.

To Mr. LA COMBE, an eminent Lawyer, on the Letters of Chriſtina Queen of Sweden, publiſhed at Paris.

S I R,   Ferney, June 13, 1765.

I .Received, the day before yeſterday, by the duthefs D'Anville, the private letters of the queen of Sweden, which you did me the honour to fend me. I am not furprifed to find how much you are ſhocked at the * aſſaſſination of her gentleman-uſher, nor at the indignation which you exprefs againſt that cruel and capricious woman.

You do other kingdoms too much honour, I am afraid, when you fay that Chriſtina

* In the gallery at Fontainbleau, for which ſhe was commanded to quit the kingdom by Lewis XIV. who held this act of hers in the utmoſt deteſtation.

would

would have been punifhed any where but in
France. Punifhed fhe would moft certainly
have been, in countries where juftice and the
laws prefide ; but thofe countries are few in
number ; and, to fpeak the real truth, I know
of no place where they are ftrictly obferved.
This woman, wicked as fhe was, might moft
affuredly have remained with impunity at
Rome, Madrid, or Vienna, and in fhort in
any place where one man extinguifhes all
laws, and money is the only God.

I fhould be greatly oblifhed to you for any
intelligence with regard to the authenticity
of thefe letters. I have publifhed fome of
Henry IVth's in the new edition of my *General Hiftory*, which are extremely curious,
which I did from the love I bear to the memory of that illuftrious hero, the only monarch of France, who was an honour to human nature, who is intitled to our bleffings,
our regret, and our everlafting remembrance
of him. I am obliged for thefe divine letters
to Mr. La Mothe, who copied them at An-
douin from the original. I am yet to learn
whether

whether the letters of Chriftina were written in Italian, and tranflated by you into French; and am forry to find in them the words *pompous* and *calotins*, which have been adopted into our language within my own memory.

If the letters are really Chriftina's, it might not be improper to obferve, that a perfon who abdicates a· crown on purpofe to run about, and fee the world, ought at leaft to he wife; and even if we fuppofe her obliged to write with all that imprudent pride, we fhall be apt·more to condemn than to pity her, It had been very eafy for this princefs to have acquired glory whilft fhe was on the throne: the daughter of Guftavus might have been adored, even if fhe had done nothing but common things, like other princes, the reputation of her father was fo great, that the people would readily have made allowance for all the follies of her fex, and even for all the mifchief which fhe might have done if fhe had dared. Thofe muft be born without the leaft fhare either of wit or vir-

s   virtue

virtue who can't fhine upon a throne, and immortalize themfelves by what are called good actions, which by the way are much more eafily performed than fuch as are truly great and noble.

The book, however, is a valuable relict, and may ferve at leaft as an example to other princes, who may have the fame foolifh defire to abdicate. I thank you for the prefeut, and hope you will endeavour to clear up my doubts concerning it.

I have the honour to be,

Sir, your's, &c.

LETTER XIX.

To the Sieur FEZ, Bookfeller at Avignon.

IN your letter from Avignon, dated April 30, you propofe to fell me, for a thoufand crowns, the whole edition of a collection of Voltaire's miftakes, both with regard to maxims and hiftorical facts, which you tell me you printed in the pope's dominions. I think myfelf in confcience obliged to inform you, that in compofing a new edition of my works, I have difcovered, in the firft, above two thoufand crowns worth of errors, and as in quality of author, I have probably miftaken about one half on my own fide; this you fee would amount to at leaft twelve thoufand livres; fo that I fhould cheat you of nine thoufand francs. Obferve moreover what you get on the account of maxims; this is an affair particularly interefting to all the powers engaged in war, from the Baltic to Gibraltar; I am not therefore in the leaft furprifed

when

when you inform me, that the work is univerfally fought after.

General Laudon, and the whole Livres.
imperial army, cannot poffibly take
lefs than thirty thoufand copies,
which you will fell at forty fous a
piece; that you know is   -   60000

The king of Pruffia, who is paf-
fionately fond of maxims, and more
bufy about them at prefent than
ever, will help you off with nearly
the fame quantity, which will be   60000

You may depend alfo on prince
Ferdinand ; for I always obferved,
when I had the honour of paying
my refpects to him, he was happy
in finding out my miftakes of this
kind ; you may therefore put him
down, for twenty thoufand,   -   40000
                                      ‾‾‾‾‾‾‾‾‾‾
                                       160000

H   Brought

Brought over   160000

With regard to the French army,
where they talk more French than
the Auſtrians and Pruſſians put together; you may ſend them at leaſt
a hundred thouſand copies, which,
at forty ſous each, will amout to   200000

In England and the colonies,
where theſe iſlanders ſtudy from
morning till night to find out my
miſtakes, and turn them to their
own advantage, you may hope at
leaſt to diſpoſe of a hundred thouſand,   -   -   -   200000

As to monks and divines,
who deal particularly in this kind
of ware, you can't ſet them down
at leſs, in all parts of Europe, than
a hundred thouſand, which makes
in all,   -   -   -   600000
                                        ————————
                                        1160000

Brought

Brought over 1160000

Add to this lift about a hundred
thoufand lovers of the dogmatic
amongft the laity,   -   -   200000

1360000

Sum-total one million three hundred and
fixty thoufand livres, which you will touch
at one ftroke, from which, fome little expence being dedu&ed, the net produce re-
maining for you will be at leaft one million.

I cannot therefore fufficiently admire your
difintereftednefs, in facrificing fo large a fum
to me, on paying down only three thoufand
livres. The only thing which could prevent
my accepting your propofal would be the fear
of offending Mr. Inquifitor of the faith, or
for the faith, who no doubt has given you
his imprimatur, for certain maffes which he
will fay for you; that is, if you pay him ho-
neftly for them. This fan&ion once given,

muft

muſt not be given in vain ; the faithful muſt
rejoice in it, and I ſhould be afraid of excom-
munication, were I to ſupprefs an edition ſo
uſeful, approved by a Jacobine, and printed
at Avignon.

* As to your anonymous author, who
has dedicated his evening vigils to this important work, I admire his modeſty. I beg
my beſt compliments to him, as well as to
your ink-merchant.

I am, in hopes of becoming better, and
acknowledging my faults with all humility,
yours, &c.

* Though Mr. Voltaire (ſays the French editor) diverts himſelf thus agreeably with his own
miſtakes, he was not much pleaſed at the diſco-
very of ſo many blunders, anachroniſms, and
contradiƈtions, which Mr. Berthier and others
found out in his Univerſal Hiſtory.

LETTER XX.

To the King of P R U S S I A *, on his Recovery.

IN Pluto's dark abodes, the fifters three,
Who weave too faft the threads of deftiny,
As 'long the Styx they took their ev'ning
    walk,
Had often heard the wand'ring fpirits talk
Of Pruffia's gallant deeds, the laws he made,
The wars he fought, the viitues he difplay'd.
As thus they trac'd the hero from his birth,
They took him for the oldeft king on earth ;
And as his wond'rous acts they counted o'er,
Inftead of forty, wrote him down fourfcore.

---

* This very pretty complimentary letter is not
to be met with in the new edition of Voltaire's
works, and was never printed before, though
written above fifteen years ago. The thought
is well carried on; but the poem ends flatly and
abruptly.

Then Atropos, to kings a hateful name,
Difpatch'd by gloomy Dis, to Berlin came;
Her fatal fhears prepar'd, expecting there
To find a poor old man, with filver hair,
And wrinkled forehead :—Great was her
    furprize,
To fee his auburn locks, and fparkling eyes;
To fee him wield the fword, to hear him
    play
On the foft flute, his jovial roundelay.
She call'd to mind how once Alcides great,
And fmooth-tongu'd Orpheus, brav'd the
    pow'r of fate;
She trembled when fhe faw, in Pruffia join'd,
The voice of Orpheus, with Alcides' mind;
Affrighted, threw her fatal fhears afide,
And home returning, to her fifters cry'd,
For Pruffia weave a new and golden thread,
Lafting as that for god-like Lewis made.
In the fame caufe did both the heroes fight;
'Gainft the fame foes with equal zeal unite.
Both gain'd by wond'rous acts immortal
    fame;
The fame their valour, and their end the
    fame;

And

And both hereafter ſhall — but ſoft ; the muſe
No longer the unequal taſk purſues ;
Two living monarchs aptly to deſign,
Requires an abler pen, and ſtronger pow'rs
    than mine.

LET-

LETTER XXI.

To Mr. RO·USSEAU*, of Touloufe, Director of the Encyclopædian Journal, printed at Bouillon, concerning a letter inferted in the St. James's Chronicle, July, 1762.

SIR,   Ferney, Oct. 16, 1762.

I N anfwer to yours of Auguft 14, for which I am greatly obliged to you, I muft inform you, that the duke of Grafton, who has been in my neighbourhood for fome time paft, fhewed me, in the *St. James's Chronicle*, a latter attributed to me; but apparently the produce of Grub-ftreet, or the charnel-

---

*There were at this time at Paris three Rouffeaus; Mr. Rouffeau of Touloufe; the celebrated John Baptift Rouffeau, an eminent poet; and the famous John James Rouffeau of Geneva, equally diftinguifhed for his extraordinary abilities, his ingenious paradoxes, and the perfecutions which he has fuffered from bigotry and enthufiafm.

houfe

houfe of St. Innocent. I muſt be obliged, out of regard to my character, to contradict this impertinent rhapſody in all the Engliſh papers. Men of ſenſe and candor know what credit is to be given to idle reports of this kind, which the public is overrun with, and heartily tired of.

With regard to the German critique on my *Hiſtory of Peter the Great*, I ſhall be glad to ſee it in your Journal. Thoſe remarks, which are ſenſible and judicious, will be of ſervice to me in the ſecond volume. I may very probably be miſtaken in ſome points, though I have followed as nearly as I could the memoirs ſent me from * Peterſburg.

There was a groſs error in the manuſcript concerning religion ; the patriarch Nicholas was miſtaken for the patriarch Photius,

---

* The French editor tells us, in a note on this paſſage, that Mr. Voltaire's *Hiſtory of Peter the Great* is nothing but a Gazette, and that it was written by him merely to conciliate the favour of the court of Ruſſia.

H. 5.   who

who lived an hundred years before him. This
has been corrected in feveral copies. In another place, Apraxin is put for Narifkin.
As to matters of fact, if they are contefted,
the archives of Peterfburgh muft anfwer for
me. My *Hiftory of Charles* XII. was fe-
verely criticifed ; the criticifms are forgotten,
the hiftory remains.

LETTER XXII.

To Mr. ROUSSEAU, of Touloufe.

SIR,

YOU wrote to me fome time ago concerning a letter, as ridiculous as it was inju-
rious, printed in my name, in the Englifh
Monthly Review for June ; I then fignified to
you both my refentment and contempt of this
very vifible impofture ; but as fome very
refpectable characters are attacked in this
letter, it is of confequence that the author
fhould be difcovered : I therefore hereby promife a reward of fifty louis-d'ors to any one
who will convict him, &c.

LETTER XXIII.

To Mr. de la FARGUE, a Poet, who had addreſſed ſome verſes to him.

SIR,

THE leſs I deſerve your elegant verſes, the more I am pleaſed with them. Beauties receive the compliments paid them with in-difference; the homely are delighted with them. I would have anſwered you in ſome verſes of my own, if I had not been ſo deeply engaged in thoſe of Corneille. Every moment that I ſpare from my commentary on the works of that great man, is a robbery of him. I cannot, however, deny myſelf the pleaſure of thanking you, and ſaying with how much eſteem I have the honour to be,

Sir, yours, &c.

LETTER XXIV.

From Mr. VOLTAIRE's Secretary to the Secretary of Mr. le FRANC de POMPIGNAN.

SIR,

YOU wrote three letters to Mr. de Voltaire, figned Ladouz, at the Hotel des Afturies, wherein you inform him that you had been fecretary to the famous Mr. le Franc de Pompignan; but that you have no longer the honour to belong to him, being difmiffed on a fufpicion of having furnifhed Mr. de Voltaire with memoirs againft him. The falfity of this you defired Mr. Voltaire to atteft. His anfwer was, that he knew nothing of you, nor you of him; and that he never received any memoirs againft Mr. le Franc de Pompignan but his own works, which being himfelf old, infirm, and almoft blind, he has now commiffioned me to repeat to you.

This

This then is the fubftance of all he knows concerning Mr. le Franc de Pompignan.

1. Some very indifferent verfes.

2. An oration before the academy, in which he infults all men of genius and letters.

3. A memorial to the king, wherein he informs his majefty, that he has an excellent library at Pompignan.

4. The defcription of a fine feaft, which he made at Pompignan, and the proceffion in which he marched behind a young Jefuit, accompanied by all the bagpipes in the country; with an account of a treat of fix and twenty covers, which was talked of all over the province.

5. A fine fermon of his own compofing, where he tells us, that he was with the ftats in the firmament, whilft the preachers of

Paris,

Paris, and all the men of letters, ftood below in the mire.

6. A fine wife, very rich, very devout,
and very amiable, who cries night and
morning for the lofs of her dear friends the
faithful Ignatians, who has brought the
fignor de Pompignan, her worthy fpoufe, a
fon and heir, and who is now very forry fhe
was made to believe that fhe had married
an Apollo, &c.

My mafter has likewife been informed,
that Mr. le Franc de Pompignan (though he
is drowned) compared himfelf to Mofes,
and his brother the bifhop to Aaron; he
defircs his compliments to them.

He has alfo heard talk of a paftoral
of the bifhop's, addrefled to the inhabitants
of Puy, in Velai, by Mr. Cortiat, fecretary.
He is told, that in this paftoral mention is
made of Ariftophanes, Diogenes, the Encyclopœdia, Fontenelle, la Motte, Perrault,
Terraffon,

Tertaſſon, Boindin, Bacon, Deſcartes, Malle-branche, Lock, Newton, Leibnitz, Monteſ-quieu, &c. We congratulate the gentleman of Puy in Velai, on having peruſed all theſe writers : like maſter, like man ; but Mr. Voltaire enters into none of theſe ſcientific ſquabbles : he tills his land, and leaves to great men the honour of enlightening the age they live in.

You acquaint him that the biſhop of Alais will take you for his ſecretary, provided you can get an atteſtation in due form that you never betrayed the ſecrets of Mr. le Franc de Pompignan ; this atteſta-tion he readily ſends you, and hopes that when you are ſettled at Alais, you will not be like the ſecretary Cortiat.

I am, Sir,.

Whatever you pleaſe to ſtile me, &c. &c.

P. S.

P. S. I afk pardon, Sir; I had forgot to mention, amongft the works of Mr. de Pompignan, the Deift's Prayer, which he has elegantly tranflated from the Englifh into excellent French, and in a fine modern ftile.

LETTER XXV.

To Mr. ROUSSEAU, Director of the
Encyclopœdian Journal.

S I R,   Paradife, near Geneva,
                                        Nov. 19, 1764.

IT is very true, as you obferve in your
letter of the 4th inftant, that there is always
fomething coming out in my name, as people often give you made wines inftead of
foreign ones. The venders of this merchan-
dize deceive themfelves more than the public.
My wines have always been but indifferent,
and thofe who put my name will never make
a fortune.

I have been informed moreover, that they
have publifhed in Holland my private letters ;
the collection, I believe in reality to be very
private ; for the public will know nothing
of it. I cannot indeed help thinking but
that it is an affront to the public, aad a viola-
tion

tion of all the laws of fociety, to publifh any man's letters in his life-time without his confent; but to impute to him fuch as he never wrote, an abominable piece of forgery *. This collection has never yet reached me; I am told it is a very bad one, and therefore give myfelf no concern about it.

I prefume, that in thofe familiar letters attributed to me, not one of them will begin like that of Tully's, " I fhall be glad to

---

* Mr. Voltaire wrote feveral letters, wherein he difclaimed the *Pucelle* and the *Dictionaire Philofophique*. The letter before us is full of contradictions and falfe modefty: he avows and difavows at the fame time the private letters printed at Amfterdam, as is evidently proved by Mr. Freron, who was fo cruelly and unjuftly treated in the *Pucelle*, and many other parts of Voltaire's works, for attacking the inconfiftency of his conduct, which Freron difcovered and reflected on, perhaps with too much feverity; but when authors quarrel, they generally treat each other like pirates. For Voltaire's real character, fee a book, much admired, entitled, *The Oracle of the new Philofophers*, by Mr. Guyon.

N. B. This note by the French editor.

hear

hear you are in good health; for myfelf,
I am perfectly well." This would evidently
be a lye in print.

I know we have the letters of Henry IV.
cardinal d'Offat, and madam de Sevigné.
Young Racine publifhed fome of his father's; they were but trifling, and were only
pardoned out of refpect to his illuftrious
name; but we are not at liberty to publifh
the correfpondence of obfcure men, unlefs
they are as agreeable, like the *epiftolæ obfcurorum
virorum*. What entertainment can the public expect from a few ufelefs infipid letters,
written by a man retired from the world, to
people whom the world know nothing of?
It is as ill-advifed a thing to print fuch ftuff,
as it is ridiculous to read it; for which reafon all this kind of frippery finks into eternal
oblivion within a fortnight. Our modern
publications refemble the innumerable quantity of flies, that, after buzzing a few days,
perifh, and give place to others, who quickly
undergo the fame fate.

Few

Few of our occupations indeed are of much
more value or confequence; and he was no
fool who firſt faid that all was vanity, ex‐
cept the peaceable enjoyment of ourſelves.
What I have faid would deferve a place in
your journal, if it was adorned by your own
pen.

I am, Sir, &c.

LETTER XXVI.

To Mad. DUFIDAN, a Lady celebrated
for her Wit and Underſtanding.

WE both, ſo heav'n decrees, have loſt our
eyes,
Voltaire the weak, and Dufidan the wiſe.
And where's the mighty loſs? No more we
ſee
The ſons of folly, pride, and treachery,
Who, drunk with power, lord it o'er man-
kind;
Nay, in this little world we all are blind.
The city and the court, the great, the ſmall,
Fortune, and Love, and Plutus govern all;
And all are blind, like us, if, out of five,
One ſenſe alone we loſe; but few alive,
With ages like our own, can boaſt the ſame.
We live, we think, have honours, friends,
and fame;

3   And

And many a pope have seen, and many a
  king ;
Besides, you know, for so the poets sing,
Great Epicurus said, The gift of heav'n
Was a sixth sense, which wou'd alone be giv'n
To its choice fav'rites, well worth all the
  rest ;
But were the soul of perfect light possest,
We'd better then, my friend, have kept our
  eyes,
Ev'n though we cou'd not see without our
  spectacles.

  You see, madam, I am a worthy brother,
and bused in the affairs of our little an-
tient republic, few of us being less than
ninety. You tell me people are not so
agreeable as they were formerly; yet the
partridges have the same flavour as they
had in our youth, and the flowers the same
beauty; but it is not so with mankind : the
foundation of every thing is the same ; but
talents are not so : the talent of making our-
selves amiable, which has always been an uncommon one, degenerates like others. It is
not you who are changed, but it is the court,
                            and

and the city, as I hear by thofe who know them. The reafon perhaps is, we have not fufficiently ftudied the art of pleafing by Moncreif: we are employed about nothing but the fafhionable follies of the age.

Reafon gains credit flowly, and with pain. How do you think fociety can be agreeable with all that pedantic rubbifh that perpetually furrounds it! You certainly deferve the compliment of a Pucelle: one of your good things is quoted in the notes to that theological work; but at prefent you muft know it is impoffible to bring any printed book from foreign parts to Paris. Even the minifter whom you mention will not permit me to fend any thing under his cover, or directed to him. They are frightened, and I don't know why. Be contented, and if, in a fortnight's time, I don't fend you my Joan by fome honeft traveller, tell Mr. Prefident Hainault he muft furnifh you with one by means of fome hawker or other. It will coft you three livres, and is a very cheap book of divinity.

I am

I am forry your friend fhould be fo hunted; you muft have lefs of his company, and it is a great lofs to you both. I fpend my life pleafantly enough in my retreat, and with the family I have got about me. Adieu, my dear friend; take courage, and let us make a virtue of neceffity. Do you know this is a proverb taken from Cicero?

I LET.

LETTER XXVII.

To King STANISLAUS, at Luneville.

SIR,   Paradife, April 15, 1760.

I Have nothing but thanks to return your majefty; you are known indeed but by your benevolence, which has gained you the noble title you poffefs. You inftruct the world; you adorn, you relieve, you direct it, both by precept and by example. I have endeavoured at a diftance to profit from both as much as I could. We fhould all endeavour to do as much good in proportion, as your majefty does in your kingdom. You have built fine royal churches, I raife village fteeples : Diogenes removed his tub, when the Athenians equipped their fleets. Whilft you relieve a thoufand poor diftreffed wretches, we little folk muft relieve ten. It is the duty of princes and of private men, every one according to his condition, to do as much good as he can. Your majefty's laft book, which brother Menou tranfmitted to me by your order, is a new favour conferred on mankind. If any atheifts there be in this world, which I do not believe, your book will confute their impious abfurdity. The philofophers of our age have happily removed all your majefty's fufpicions on that head, and rendered your labours unneceflary. They .blefs God that, fince Newton and Défcartes, no atheift has ever appeared in Europe. You have likewife admirably well refuted thofe who formerly believed that chance had contributed towards the formation of the univerfe. Your majefty muft with the greateft pleafure obferve, that there is not a philofopher amongft us who does not confider the word itfelf as intirely void of all fenfe and meaning. The greater progrefs natural and experimental philofophy have made amongft us, the more vifibly do we perceive in every thing the hand of the Moft High.

The philofophy of our days is full of refpect for the deity. It doth dot content

itfelf

itfelf with a barren worfhip alone ; but ex-
tends its influence over our manners, and
makes our philofophers the beft of citizens
alfo. They love their country and their king,
fubmit to the laws, and fet examples of loy-
alty and obedience. They condemn to fhame
and infamy thofe pedantic and furious fac-
tions, which are equally prejudicial to the
royal prerogative, and the peace and happinefs of the fubject ; nor is there, I believe,.
one of them who would not gladly contri-
bute half his fortune to the fupport of the
kingdom. Continue, Sir, to countenance
and protect them by your authority, and
by your eloquence to convince the world
that men cannot be truly happy ; but
when kings are philofophers, and have a
number of fubjects who are philofophers alfo.
Encourage, by your powerful voice, thofe
citizens who teach nothing in their writings
and converfation but the love of God, their
king, and their country. Confound and deftroy at the fame time thofe mad and factious
fools, who accufe every man of atheifm that
is not of their opinion in matters the moft
indifferent.

The

The angelic doctor afferts, that all the Jefuits are atheifts, becaufe they won't allow the court of Pekin to be idolaters; and Hardouin the Jefuit tells us, that Pafcal, Arnauld, and Nicole muft be atheifts, becaufe they would not be Molinifts. Brother Berthier fufpects the author of the General Hiftory of the fame crime, becaufe he does not agree that the Neftorians, conducted by the blue clouds, came from the country of Jacin, in the feventh century, to build Neftorian churches at China. Brother Berthier ought to have known that the clouds conduct nobody to Pekin, and that we ought not to mix old wive's fables with facred truths. A Briton, fome years ago, making fome enquiries about the city of Paris, was accufed by the abbé de Trublet and Co. of irreligion, on account of the ftreet Tireboudin, and the ftreet Trouffe Vache; and the Briton was obliged to fettle the affair with his accufer at the Chatelet de Paris.

Kings look down with contempt on thefe little diffentions; they confult the general

good,

good, whilst their subjects, enraged one against the other, are always doing private wrongs. A great king, Sir, like your majesty, is neither Jansenist, nor Molinist; he makes reason respectable, and faction ridiculous. He makes even Jesuits good at Lorrain, in spite of themselves. When they are driven out of Portugal, he gives twelve thousand livres a year, a good house, and a convenient cave to our dear brother Menou, that once a year he may have it in his power to serve the friends under his protection. He knows that virtue and religion consist in good morality, and not in contention. He gains a blessing from all, while calumniators are universally detested.

I call to mind, Sir, with the greatest and most respectful acknowledgement, the happy hours which I have passed in your palace, and remember well that you condescended to be the delight of private company, with as much ease as you create public felicity; and that if it is a happiness to be your subject, it is a still greater happiness to be admitted as

your

your friend. I fincerely wifh, that a life fo
ufeful to the world may be extended beyond
the ordinary limits. Aureng-Zeb and Muley-
Ifhmael lived to above the age of a hundred
and five. If God granted fuch length of days
to the infidel princes, what will he not do
for Staniflaus the Beneficent?

I am, Sir, with the moft profound refpect,

yours, &c. &c.

14   L E T-

LETTER XXVIII.

To Mr. LE BRUN *, Secretary to his
Serene Highnefs the Prince of Conti, who
had fent Mr. Voltaire a fine Ode on Corneille, and was the firft who recommended
the niece to, and brought her acquainted
with him.

Ferney, Nov. 5, 1760.

I Should have made you wait at leaft thefe
four months, if I had pretended to anfwer
you in as good verfes as your own; I muft

* Mr. Le Brun was the firft man of letters
who entered warmly into the caufe of Mr. Corneille. Mr. Voltaire very generoufly embraced
the opportunity of fupporting a family which had
been left in great diftrefs by their relation Mr.
de Fontenelle, who intirely neglected them.
Freron, about this time, not knowing any thing
of Voltaire's intention, applied to the comedians,
and got a benefit in favour of Corneille's nephew. What Voltaire has done fince, is well
known. It was a noble thing in him to portion
her out from the profits of her uncle's works:
that

therefore content myfelf with telling you in plain profe, that I admire both your ode and your propofal. It is fit that an old foldier of the great Corneille's fhould endeavour to be ferviceable to the grand-daughter of his general; but when we are building caftles and churches, and have relations to provide for, we can't do all we would wifh to do for a perfon who ought to be affifted by the greateft people in the kingdom.

I am old, Sir, but have a niece with me who is a lover of the arts, and has made a proficiency in fome of them. If the lady you mention, and whom I fuppofe you are acquainted with, will accept of fuch an education as my niece can afford her, fhe will take care of her as of a daughter, and I will endeavour myfelf to be a father to her: her own need not be at any expence, and her

that edition, with other prefents, got in the whole above fixty thoufand livres. To Voltaire in a great meafure was owing alfo the reverfion of the fentence againft the family of Calas. When the chara&er of Voltaire is canvaffed, thefe actions fhould not be forgotten.

paffage

paſſage ſhall be paid to Lyons, where ſhe may wait on Mr. Tronchin, who will furniſh her with a carriage up to my houſe, or a ſervant ſhall meet her with my equipage. If this is agreeable, I am at her ſervice, and hope to thank you to the laſt hour of my life, for procuring me the honour of doing what Mr. de Fontenelle ought to have done. Part of her entertainment ſhall be to ſee us play ſome of her grandfather's pieces, and diſcuſs the ſubjects of Cinna and the Cid.

I have the honour to remain, with all due eſteem and reſpect,

Sir, your, &c.

L E T-

LETTER XXIX.

To Mr. LE BRUN.

S I R,   Delices, Nov. 22, 1760.

IN confequence of your laft letter, on the
name of Corneille, and the merit of his de-
fcendant, as well as on account of another
which I received from her, I have refolved
to do every thing in my power to ferve her.
I flatter myfelf fhe will not be difgufted at a
retreat where fhe will fometimes meet with
men of merit, who have all the refpect for
her great uncle that is due to him. Mr. La
Leu, though an eminent notary of Paris,
who lives in your neighbourhood, will, on
fight of this letter, immediately reimburfe to
you the money advanced for the journey of
Madem. Corneille. She has no preparations
to make, as linen and proper drefs of every
kind will be provided for her on her arrival.

Mr.

Mr. Tronchuin, banker, at Lyons, will have advice of her coming, and will be ready to receive, and conduct her to me. As you are so obliging as to enter willingly into this little necessary business, I shall submit it intirely to your care, and depend on the interest you take in a matter that concerns a name so dear to every man of letters.

I am, Sir, with the greatest friendship and esteem,

Your, &c.

LETTER XXX.

To Mademoiſelle CORNEILLE.

MADAM,   Delices, Nov. 22, 1760.

YOUR name, your merit, and the letter you honoured me with, increaſe both in Mrs. Dennis and myſelf our impatience to receive you, and we hope to deſerve the preference you have been ſo obliging as to favour us with. I muſt inform you that we paſs ſeveral months in the year at our country houſe near Geneva, where notwithſtanding you will be accommodated with every thing neceſſary with regard to the duties of religion ; but our principal reſidence is in France, about a league off, in a very tolerable houſe, which I am building, and where you will be more commodiouſly lodged than in the place which I now write from. You will find ſufficient amuſements in both, either in work, reading, or muſic. If you have any inclination to learn hiſtory and geography, we will

2   ſend

fend for a mafter, who I doubt not will think himfelf highly honoured in teaching any thing to a niece of the great Corneille, and I fhall be ftill more fo in having you with me.

I am, with the greateft refpect,

Madam. yours, &c.

LETTER XXXI.

To Mr. the Chevalier de R——X, at Touloufe.

S I R, Delices, Sept. 20, 1760.

I AM not well enough at prefent to have as much wit as yourfelf; you take me at a difadvantage; as Waller faid to St. Evremond, you are very good to read things which I have intirely forgot; but you muft have too much fenfe not to fee that.—*Mr. Montefquieu received into the academy for having laughed at it,* is a piece of drollery, and nothing more. Do as the academy did, Sir, enter into the joke; and above all take care never to read the difcourfes of Mr. Mallet, unlefs you are troubled with a want of fleep.

You have explained very well what Montefquien meant by the word *virtue* in a republic; but if you recollect that the Dutch broiled upon a gridiron the hearts of the two

De

De Wits; if you call to mind how my good neighbours the Swifs fold duke Lewis Sforfa for a little ready money; if you remember that the republican John Calvin, that worthy divine, after having maintained in his writings that no man fhould ever be perfecuted, not even thofe who denied the Trinity, burned alive with green fagots a Spaniard who differed with him in opinion on that fubject, you will moft certainly conclude, that there is no more virtue in a republic than in a monarchy.

Ubicunque calculum ponas, ibi naufragium fere invenies.

The world, my friend, is one great fhipwreck : and man's motto, " Save yourfelf if you can."

I am forry I faid that William the Conqueror difpofed of the lives and fortunes of his new fubjects like an eaftern monarch : you did right in condemning me for it : I fhould only have faid, he abufed his victory,

as

as they always do, both in the eaft and in the weft; for moft indifputable it is, that no monarch upon earth has a right to divert himfelf with plundering and killing his fub-jeēts juft as he thinks proper. We poor hif-torians are too often believed, and the greateft injury we can do mankind is to tell them, as fome do, that the princes of the eaft are very welcome to cut off as many heads as they pleafe. It might very probably happen, that the oriental princes and their confeffors might imagine this noble prerogative was by divine right. I have feen many travellers who had paffed through Afia, who all fhrugged up their fhoulders when you talked to them of this pretended defpotifm independent of the laws. It is true, indeed, that in trou-blefome times, both the monarchs and mi-nifters of the eaft are as wicked as our Lewis XI. or Alexander VI. True alfo it is that men are every where equally inclined to violate the laws, when they are angry, and there is no great difference in this refpeē from Ireland to Japan. There are, notwith-ftanding, in every place fome honeft men,

and

and virtue, improved by fcience, turns the hell of this world into a paradife.

Your virtue, Sir, as appears by your letter, is of this kind; and the illuftrious prefident Montefquieu would have found in you a friend worthy of him.

A gentleman, whofe eftate lies, I believe, not far from you, is now with me, and propofes fpending fome time in my little retreat; it is the Marquis d' Argent. He has convinced me that nothing can be more amiable than a man of honour and virtue, who has wit and genius. I could wifh you would do me the fame honour, and affure you it would be the greateft happinefs to him, who with all refpect and efteem is,

Sir, yours, &c.

P. S. You will pardon my not having wrote this with my own hand.

LETTER XXXII.

To Mr. HALLER, a celebrated Philofopher and Poet of Switzerland.

SIR,

I Send you a little certificate, which may
ferve to acquaint you with the character of
Graffet, for whom your immediate protection
is warmly folicited. This fellow publifhed
at Laufanne an infamous libel againft morality, religion, the peace of individuals, and
the good order of fociety. It will become a
man of your worth and abilities to deny a
wretch like him that favour and protection,
which fhould only be referved for the good
and virtuous. I fhall depend on your
kindnefs and on your juftice in this particular.
Pardon this fcrap of paper; it is not agreeable, I know, to the ufage of Germany,

but

but it fuits the franknefs of a Frenchman, who has a greater refpect for you than any German.

One Lerveche, formerly preceptor to Mr. Conftant, is the author of a libel againft the late Mr. Saurin; he is minifter of a village fomewhere near Laufanne. He has wrote me two or three * letters in your name. Thefe fellows are fet of wretches very unworthy the honour of being folicited for to a man of your merit and confequence †.

* The original is " Deux ou trois lettres ano- " nymes fous votre nom." Two or three *anony- mous* letters in your name.

This feems to be a kind of bull of Mr. Vol- taire's, as one cannot well conceive how the let- ters figned with Mr. *Haller's* name could be pro- perly called *anonymous*.

† This letter, fays the French editor, full of revenge and difquietude called for the elegant and fenfible anfwer of the celebrated and inefti- mable rebublican Mr. Haller, which we have therefore with great pleafure tranfcribed. It will let us into the ftrange and unaccountable character of Mr. de Voltaire.

I take

I take this opportunity to aſſure you of the great eſteem and reſpect which I ſhall always have for you.

I am, Sir, &c.

LETTER XXXIII.

Mr. HALLER's Anfwer to Mr. de VOLTAIRE.

SIR,

YOUR letter has given me the greateſt concern. I fee and admire a gentleman poſ-ſeſſed of riches and independency, who has it in his power to chooſe the beſt company, equally applauded by monarchs and by the public, and immortalized by fame; and ſhall I behold this very man loſing all his peace and quiet, only in endeavouring to prove, that one man has ſtolen from him, and * an-other is not yet convinced whether he has or no?

---

* In ſpite of the memorial and certificate (ſays the French editor) which Mr. Voltaire procured from the ſieur Cramer, nothing could be done; though his enemies might probably have advanced ſomething againſt him not ſtrictly true : but Mr. Voltaire always ſhewed too keen a reſentment of the trifles which were written againſt him, as wit-neſs his affair with Freron.

Providence holds an equal balance to all
mankind; it has fhoweied down riches and
glory upon you. You muft have your mif-
fortunes alfo, and it has found out the equal
poife againft your happinefs, by giving you
too much fenfibility.

The perfon whom you complain of would
lofe very little by lofing the protection of a
man, who has long laid hidden is an obfcure
corner of the world, and who is happy in
having no influence or connections. The
laws alone have here power to protect the
citizen and the fubject. Mr. Graffet has the
care of my library. I have feen Mr. Lerveche,
(you mean Laroche) with one Mr. May, an
exile, whom I have vifited fometimes fince
his difgrace, and who paffed the latter part
of his time with this minifter.

If either of them have put my name to
their letters, and made people believe, that
we are more intimate than we really are, I
fhall certainly, when I fee them, refent it as
an injury done to me, which from too great
a friend-

a friendſhip for me you ſeem to have exagge-
rated.

If wiſhes had any power, I would add
one to the bleſſings you enjoy. I would
wiſh you that tranquillity which flies before
genius, which perhaps is not of ſo great
value when conſidered with relation to ſociety, but of infinitely more with regard to
ourſelves ; the moſt celebrated man in Europe
would then be alſo the moſt happy.

I am, Sir,

Your perfect admirer, &c.

LET-

(193)

LETTER XXXIV.

To Mr. BELLOY, Author of the
Siege of Calais, a Tragedy, reprefented
in February, 1765.

SIR,

I AM almoft blind, but have ftill my hear-
ing, and the voice of fame has acquainted
me with your aftonifhing fuccefs. I have
a heart alfo that is interefted in it : permit
me to join, though at fo great a diftance, my
warm applaufe, with that of the * whole

---

* All Paris, fays the French editor, crouded
with rapture to this excellent tragedy, fo interefting to every lover of his country. The city of
Calais fignalized themfelves more particularly by
the marks of favour fhewn both to the tragedy
and the author of it. He was crowned for
the firft time, and the applaufe of the court
equalled that of the city. Nothing lefs than
gold was given to Mr. Belloy. A medal was
ftruck at the Louvre; one fide of it reprefents

K   the

kingdom. Long and uninterrupted may be
your merit and your happinefs! Nothing

the king, with thefe words, *Artium parens*; on
the reverfe, is Apollo holding a flag, on which
is written Corneille, Racine, Moliere; and a
little below,

Et qui nafcetur ab illis.

An æra glorious for the poets, and which at the
fame time does honour to the monarch, who
fhews fuch tafte and love for genius and abilities.

The extraordinary, tho' deferved fuccefs of this
tragedy, excited the malice of fome little poets,
who wrote epigrams againft the author and his
piece.

Epigram, on the Siege of Calais.

Bombaft and fuftian all, a deal
Of idle prate, and foolifh zeal;
A heap of flattery, great pretence,
With very little wit or fenfe:
Such was the merits join'd to raife it,
And fuch are all the fools who praife it.

Another, on the fame.

Rejoice, ye knaves and fools, I fay, rejoice.
All citizens enroll'd by public voice.

A glo-

remains to crown your glory but to be abuſed
by Freron.

I embrace you without ceremony, which,
with brother poets, is unneceſſary. I am,
with great pleaſure and ſincerity,

Yours, &c.

A glorious honour, which, in Lewis' reign,
Who ſav'd their country only cou'd obtain.
Of old 'twas dearly bought!—but now-a-days
'Tis to be had for—praiſing Belloy's plays.

There follows, in this place, an epigram, as it
is called in the original, on the picture of Mr.
Belloy; but it is ſo poor a piece, that it is not
worth tranſlating. And likewiſe another on the
word _ſiege_, which, in French, ſignifies both _ſiege_
and _ſeat_; but, as the pun does not anſwer in
Engliſh, it could not be tranſlated.

K 2   L E T-

LETTER XXXV.

PARODY of Mr. VOLTAIRE's Letter to BELLOY.

BLIND tho' I am, my friend, I ftill can
  hear
The voice of fame, which thunders in my
  ear,
And talks for ever of thy charming lays,
Which make ev'n malice fmile, and envy
  praife.
The patriot and the poet all commend;
Whoe'er is Belloy's muft be France's friend.
Equall'd by few, by fewer ftill furpafs'd,
Long may thy merit, long thy praifes laft.
One honour ftill remains, and one alone,
To crown thy fame, the cenfure of Freron.
Whilft I from envy, pride, and malice free,
Who look not on thee with bafe jealoufy,

In

In brother bards unfeemly, give thee joy;
Nor fteal we from le Franc, r poor * Rofoy.

* Mr. Du Rofoy, author of a tragedy called
the Siege of Calais, printed about two months
before the appearance of Mr. du Belloy's, was im-
prifoned at Fort l'Evigne, for endeavouring to
perfuade the public, that the players communi-
cated that piece in manufcript to Mr. du Belloy.
This young man, who is but an indifferent poet,
quarrelled with fome perfons of the firft confequence. He even went fo far as to accufe M. du
Clairon of having ftolen the manufcript of the
tragedy of Cromwell from the Sieur Morand,
who has been dead thefe ten years. Unhappily
the world, and particularly Mr. Morand's friends
believed the accufation.

N. B. This note by the French editor.

The above Parody is a very poor piece of
poetry, as well in the original as in the tranflation, and feems not to have been written by Voltaire, though inferted amongft his letters by the
French editor.

L E T-

LETTER XXXVI.

To the Marquis de VILLETTE,
Son of the Treafurer.

H OW few are thofe who teach while they
delight !
How few, like thee, who think as well as
write !
But reafon with the fifter graces join'd,
'To give thee perfect empire o'er the mind,
Thus with his lyre Apollo wins our hearts,
And kills the ferpent Pytho with his
darts.
'Tis the fame great, the fame all-pow'rful god,
Who quells the favage monfters of the
wood,
As he whofe active and enliv'ning ray,
Gives warmth to nature, and lights up the
day,

But

But more a god he is, when to the charms
Of love he yields, and fports in Daphne's
    arms.

The lefs, Sir, that the owl of Ferney deferves your fine verfes, the more ought he
to thank you for them : he interefts himfelf in every thing that concerns you, becaufe he knows your worth.

In thee we, as in others, find
The venial faults of heedlefs youth ;
But pardon foibles, where the mind
Is fraught with wifdom and with truth.

I fhall retain you as one of the beft advo-
cates for our philofophy, and I hereby give
you notice of it ; all will by and by be un-
veiled to you ; you fhall be one of us.

To be good-natur'd, eafy, gay, and free,
Is man's due tribute to fociety :
For others this ; and to ourfelves remains
The duty to be—happy for our pains.

K 4   We

We have one little new cell, and are building another. You know how much you are beloved in our convent *.

* The French editor, in a note to this letter, has given us fome very dull anecdotes concerning the marquis to whom it is addrefied, which, as they could afford no entertainment to the reader, are omitted.

L E T.

LETTER XXXVII.

To Mr. D'AMOUREUX*.

MY DEAR FRIEND, Ferney, March 1, 1765?

I Have read over with the greatest satisfaction the new memoirs of the innocent family of Calas, by Mr. Beaumont. I admired, and even shed tears over it; but I learned nothing from thence which I did not know before. I have been thoroughly convinced with regard to that point for some time past, and had the happiness of procuring the first satisfactory proofs of it.

---

* This letter, says the French editor, has been already published: we have reprinted it here, with additions, or more properly speaking, the restoration of a long passage, which was not suffered to appear in the Paris edition; we mean that part of it which concerns Mr. Rousseau of Geneva. It is so far particularly valuable, as it gives us a farther insight into the character of Mr. Voltaire, and his opinion of that celebrated philosopher.

K 5   You

You feem defirous to know how this univerfal abhorrence of it has happened, that
all Europe cries out againft this legal murder of poor Calas, broke upon the wheel at
Toulouse; and how it came to pafs that the
difcovery of this dreadful piece of injuftice
fhould take its rife in a little unknown corner of the world, between the Alps and
mount Jura, a hundred leagues diftance from
the fcene of this mournful tragedy.

About the end of March, 1762, a traveller, who had paffed through Languedoc,
came to fee me at my little retreat, two
leagues from Geneva, who acquainted me
with the punifhment of Calas; and at the
fame time affured me, that he was perfectly
innocent. I obferved to him, that it was
fcarce probable he could have committed the
crime; and ftill lefs probable that the judges,
who had no private intereft in the affair,
could condemn an innocent man to be broke
upon the wheel.

The day after, I was informed that one
of the children of this unhappy father had
taken

taken refuge in Switzerland, not far from
my little cottage. His flight inclined me to
think the family guilty. I reflected, notwithftanding, that the father had been condemned for affaffinating, without any ac-
complice, his own fon on account of his religion, and that this man was fixty-nine
years of age at the time of his death. I never remembered to have heard of any old
man who was fo horrible an enthufiaft. I
had always remarked, that this kind of religious rage feldom attacked any but young
man, whofe lively, weak, and tumultuous
imagination is frequently inflamed by fuperftition. The fanatics of the Cevennes were
all madmen of between twenty and thirty,
and taught from their infancy to ftile themfelves prophets. The convulfionifts, many
of whom I faw at Paris, were all little girls,
or young fellows; the old men in our mo-
nafteries are not fo fufceptible of furious zeal
as thofe who are juft out of their noviciate.
All the remarkable affaffins, who were armed
by fanaticifm, have been young men, as well
as thofe who pretended to be poffeffed; and
                                        I ne-

I never heard of an old man's being exor-
cifed. This confideration induced me to
doubt of his guilt; befides that, the crime
was to the laft degree unnatural.

I ordered the young man to be brought to
me, and expected to find him one of thofe
wild enthufiafts whom I have frequently
met with in his country ; inftead of which,
I faw before me a fimple lad, open and in-
genuous, with a countenance of the utmoft
foftnefs, and which at once interefted you
in his favour, and who, whilft he was
fpeaking to me, endeavoured, but in vain,
to hide the tears that fell from him. He
told me he had been apprentice to a manu-
facturer at Nifmes, where it was the public
talk that his whole family at Touloufe would
foon be condemned to death ; that all Languedoc believed them guilty ; and that, to
avoid fuch dreadful ignominy, he had fled to
Switzerland.

· I afked him if his father and mother had
the character of being paffionate and cruel ;
He

He affured me to the contrary; and that
they had never beat one of their children
in their whole lives; but on the other hand,
were the moft tender and indulgent parents.
I muft own to you this thoroughly convinced
me of their innocence. I received more information, a little after, from two merchants
at Geneva, men of undoubted probity, who
had lodged with Calas at Touloufe; they
confirmed me in my opinion. Far from
thinking the family of Calas a fet of parricides
and fanatics, I began to fee that they had
been accufed and ruined by fome vile enthufiafts. Long fince had I experienced what
the fpirit of party and calumny were capable
of.

But what was my aftonifhment, when,
on my writing to Languedoc concerning this
ftrange affair, both Catholics and Proteftants
affured me, in anfwer, that no doubt was to
be made of Calas's guilt; but I was not yet
deterred. I took the liberty to write to the
Governors of the province, and all the neigh-
bouring places, and even to the minifters
of

of ftate. All unanimoufly advifed me not to interfere any farther. Every body condemned me, and I ftill perfifted. Such, Sir, was my conduct.

The widow of Calas, from whom, to crown her misfortunes, they had taken away her daughters, was retired into folitude, to indulge her griefs, and wait for that death which fhe every day expected. I did not in-quire whether fhe was a Proteftant, but only whether fhe believed in a God, the rewarder of virtue, and the avenger of guilt. I afked her, whether in the name of that God, fhe would atteft, under her own hand, that her hufband died innocent: fhe never hefitated in the leaft; no more did I. I defired Mr. Mariette to take her defence to the king's council. Mad. Calas was obliged to leave her retreat, and undertake her journey to Paris.

We fee by this, that if there are great crimes in the world, there are perhaps as many virtues; and that if fuperftition pro-
duces

duces misfortunes, philofophy can repair them.

A lady, whofe generofity was equal to her high birth, and who had been fome time at Geneva to inoculate her daughters, was the firft that affifted this unfortunate family. Several French, who had retired into this country, contributed alfo. The Englifh travellers diftinguifhed themfelves more particularly in this affair. As Mr. Beaumont obferves, there was a conteft of generofity between the two nations, which fhould be the moft forward in fuccouring virtue thus cruelly oppreffed.

What followed no one knows better than yourfelf; who laboured in the caufe of innocence with more zeal and intrepidity ? How nobly did you encourage thofe orators who were heard by France and by all Europe with fo much attention ! It recalled to mind the times when Cicero defended Amerinus, accufed of parricide, before the fenate. Some perfons, indeed, who ftiled themfelves holy and devout, declared againft Calas; but, for

the

the firſt time ſince the eſtabliſhment of fana-
ticiſm, the voice of wiſdom put them to
ſilence.

Reaſon may now indeed be ſaid to have
gained a glorious victory amongſt us ; but
would you believe it, my dear friend ! the
family of Calas, ſo nobly aſſiſted, and ſo
well revenged, was not the only one accuſed of parricide on a religious pretext ;
not the only one who has been ſacrificed to
the rage of prejudice ; there is one which is
yet more unhappy, becauſe whilſt it experienced the ſame misfortunes, it has not met
with the ſame conſolation, or found a Mariette, a * Beaumont, and a Loiſeau.

* Mr. Beaumont, to the honour of humanity,
ſeems reſolved to defend the cauſe of the Sirvens,
as he has already done that of Calas, which I remarked to him at the time when he wrote me
this letter.

N. B. This note by the French editor, who,
according to the laſt ſentence in it, ſhould ſeem to
be the perſon to whom this letter is addreſſed, Mr.
D'Amoureux.

It

It should seem that there still dwells in Languedoc an infernal fury, brought thither in former times by the inquisitors in the train of Simon de Montfort, and that ever since those days she continues, every now and then, to shake her torch amongst us.

A lawyer of Castres, whose name was Sirven, had three daughters : as the family were Protestants, the youngest of the daughters was stolen away from her mother, put into a convent, and well whipped, to teach her her catechism : she runs mad, and throws herself into a well about a league from her father's house. The zealots immediately conclude, that the father, mother, and sisters had drowned the child. It was taken for granted amongst the Catholics of that province, that the Protestants always make it a rule for fathers and mothers to hang, drown, or cut the throats of all those children who shew any inclination towards the Romish religion. This was at the very time when the family of Calas was in prison, and the scaffold prepared for them.

The

The affair of the drowned child foou reached Toulouse. Here, said they, is a new inftance of a father and mother con-victed of parricide. The rage of the popu-lace increafed; Calas was broke upon the wheel, and a warrant iffued out againft Sir-ven, his wife, and daughter. Sirven had juft time to efcape with his fick family; they travelled on foot, and without any provifions, over cragged mountains covered with fnow. One of the daughters was brought to-bed in the midft of all the ice and cold, and dying herfelf, carried her dying infant in her arms. They bent their courfe toward Switzerland. The fame chance which conducted the chil-dren of Calas decreed that thefe alfo fhould put themfelves under my protection.

Figure to yourfelf, my friend, four fheep, whom the butchers accufe of having flain a lamb; fuch was the fight I had before me. So much innocence, joined to fo much mi-fery, it is impoffible to defcribe. What could I do? What would you have done in my fituation? Muft one be content to weep

over

over human nature ? I took the liberty to write to the firſt preſident of Languedoc, a ſenſible and good man ; but he was not at Toulouſe. By means of a friend of ours I got a placet preſented to the vicechancellor. During this time the father, mother, and two daughters were hung in effigy near Caſtres, their goods confiſcated, and not a ſhilling left to ſupport them.

Here, Sir, is a whole honeſt, virtuous, innocent family given up to beggary and ruin, and in a ſtrange country. They meet indeed with compaſſion ; but how hard it is to remain an object of compaſſion all our lives. At laſt, I am told, that a pardon ſhall be procured for them. I thought at firſt they meant the judges, and that the pardon was for them. You muſt be ſatisfied that this wretched family would rather beg their bread from door to door, and die with hunger, than ſue for the pardon of a crime they were never guilty of, and which is too horrible, were they ſo, even to deſerve it. And yet how are they to obtain juſtice ? How ſurrender them-

ſelves

felves to prifon in a country where half the
people ftill believe the murder of Calas jufti-
able ? Muft they go a fecond time to demand a new trial ? Muft they endeavour
again to excite the public pity, which the
misfortunes of Calas have already exhaufted,
and which will grow tired of always having
accufations of parricide to refute, condemned
perfons to acquit, and judges to confute ?

Are not two fuch tragical events, happen-
ing fo clofe to each other, my dear friend,
proofs of that unavoidable fatality to which
our miferable race is fubjected ? That dreadful truth, fo often told us by Homer and by
Sophocles, an ufeful one indeed, as it may
teach us patience and refignation.

Muft I add, on this occafion, that whilft
thefe aftonifhing events touched me in the
tendereft manner, and affected me to the laft
degree, a man whofe profeffion you will guefs
at by what he faid, reproached me with the
intereft I had taken in two families, that
were utter ftrangers to me. Why, faid he,
do

do you trouble yourfelf about them? Let the
dead bury the dead. To which I replied: I
have found in my defart an Ifraelite bathed
in his own blood; permit me to pour oil into
his wounds. You are a Levite; let me be
a Samaritan.

They treated me indeed like a Samaritan,
made a defamatory libel upon me, which
they called a Paftoral Letter; but it was
the work of a Jefuit, and fhould be forgotten.
The wretch did not know that I had at that
time taken a Jefuit under my protection.
Could I give a ftronger proof that we fhould
look upon our enemies as our brethren?

This melancholy madmam, formerly a
little petty citizen of Geneva, is eternally
clamouring againft me, and crying out in his
convulfions, that I perfecute and purfue him
from place to place, and, in the end, fhall
force him to hang himfelf; fo much have
I fet the minifters of the gofpel and the ma-
giftrates of the country againft both his
writings and his perfon. He writes all thefe
fine

fine things to a great lady at Paris, who admires his eloquence more than that of Cicero or Boffuet, and loves her John James * like her lap-dog. This good lady fpreads her pretty little ftories about amongft other good ladies, who tell them to the very good ladies at court, till all thefe agreeable goffips are infenfibly as it were perfuaded into a moft cordial hatred of me, either upon the ftrength of her word, or from mere idlenefs. Good God! of me, who never fo much as pronounced the name of John James four times in my life; who never read any of his melancholy reveries, becaufe I hold it as an eftablifhed maxim, that he who would live long muft always laugh; me who, for thefe ten years paft, did not know whether this Allobrogian Hercules exifted or not; who thought he had been fhut up in fome hofpital, or wedged into the trunk of fome old tree in the fublime forefts of philofophic Switzerland.

* John James Rouffeau, the celebrated writer and philofopher, fo well known by his New Eloifa, &c. now in England.

Your

Your paffions are humanity, love of truth, and hatred of calumny. Conformity of character produced our friendfhip. I have fpent my life in fearching for and publifhing that truth which I revere; what other modern hiftorian has defended, the memory of a great prince againft the fhameful impoftures of an * obfcure writer, whom one may properly ftile the calumniator of kings, minifters, and generals, and who notwithftanding is no longer read?

I have done nothing more therefore with regard to the dreadful calamities of Calas and Sirven, than what every other man would have done, followed the bent of my own inclination. The aim of a philofopher is not to lament the wretched, but to ferve them.

* Mr. Voltaire, according to the French editor, alludes to the memoirs of Mad. Maintenon, by Mr. de la Beaumelle, an author who had treated Mr. Voltaire, in feveral of his performances, with great feverity.

I know

I know the rage with which fanaticifm would perfecute philofophy, whofe daughters, truth and toleration, fhe would deftroy, as fhe did poor Calas; whilft Philofophy only wifhes to difarm the children of fanaticifm, falfhood and perfecution.

Thofe who are not able to reafon, have always endeavoured to difcredit thofe who are. They have confounded the philofopher with the fophift, and miferably deceive themfelves. The true philofopher will fometimes indeed fhew his indignation againft that calumny which purfues him: he may overwhelm in eternal infamy the bafe, mercenary, hireling fcribler, who twice in the month affronts truth, reafon, tafte, and virtue. He may, as he goes along, facrifice to ridicule and contempt thofe who infult literature even in the fanctuary, where they ought moft to revere it; but at the fame time he is a ftranger to cabals, party-prejudice, and revenge. He ftudies with the wife

Montbar,

Montbar *, and the philofopher of † Voré, to
make the earth more fertile, and its inhabitants more happy. He clears the lands that
are uncultivated, increafes the number of
ploughs, and confequently of men alfo;

' * Author of an excellent work, intitled *Na ural
Hiſtory*.

† The celebrated Helvetius, author of the
Livre de l'Efprit, or *A Treatiſe on the Faculties of
the Mind*. The moft humane and generous creature upon earth. The inhabitants of Voré, where
he lived, are continually blefling and praying
for him. He was perfeeuted and banifhed on
account of his treatife. The hypocrites and devotees of the court, thofe cruel and vindictive
fpirits, confpired to deftroy him ; but the public,
which always does juftice to virtue and abilities,
. have amply repaid him for the injuries and contempt which he met with at court.

Such, adds the French editor, was alfo the fate
of the fublime Mirebeau, who fell a victim to
fixty tax-gatherers of France, who procured an
order to imprifon him in the caftle of Vincennes.

* This alludes moft probably to the *Année* likewife, a kind of review publifhed in France, and
fuppofed to be written by Freron.

L   employs

employs and feeds the poor, encourages ma-
trimony, relieves the orphan, never mur-
murs againſt neceſſary taxes, but enables the
huſbandman to pay them with chearfulneſs.
He expeᒼts nothing from the world, but does
in all his power to ſerve it ; abhors the hy-
pocrite, pities the ſuperſtitious, and, in ſhort,
is a friend to all mankind.

I perceive I am drawing your portrait,
and that it wants nothing to make it per-
feᒼly like, but your being happy enough to
live in the country *.

* After the publication of this letter, Freron,
in his *Année*, likewiſe put out a letter from a Pro-
teſtant philoſopher, which was very ſevere both on
Calas and Voltaire, which probably gave occa-
ſion to the following letter from Mr. D'Argenu.

LETTER XXXVIII.

From the Marquis D'A R G E N U*, Brigadier General.

MY DEAR FRIEND,

I Have lately read, in a little periodical paper, called, *The Annals of Literature*, a fatire, occafioned by a piece of juftice done to the family of Calas, by the fupreme tribunal of the mafters of requefts, which has raifed the indignation of all honeft men, as I am told moft of thefe papers do. The author, by a very ftale device, which every body fees through, pretends that he received a letter from a Proteftant philofopher, who tells him, that if the world were to determine concerning that affair from Mr. Voltaire's letter, which has circulated over Europe, they

* We are informed by whom, but not to whom, this letter was written; but may conjecture it was moft probably addreffed to the French editor.

would

would entertain but a very falfe idea of it.
The author of the paper does not venture
directly to attack the mafters of requefts ; but
feems to hope his cenfure of Voltaire will
fall upon them, as they all proceeded on the
fame evidence.

He begins by endeavouring to deftroy that
favourable prefumption which all the lawyers
went upon, that it was not natural to fuppofe a father fhould affaffinate his fon, merely on a fuppofition of his being inclined
to change his religion. He oppofes to this
argument, the validity of which is fo univerfally acknowledged, the example of Junius
Brutus, fuppofed to have condemned his
fon to death, and is fo blind as not to fee
that Junius Brutus was a judge, who with
the greateft concern facrificed nature to duty.
What kind of comparifon can there be between a fevere fentence and an execrable af-
faffination ! between an act of duty and a
parricide, and fuch a parricide too ! which,
if it had been committed, the father, mother,
brother, and friend, muft all have been ac-
complices in !

He

He goes fo far as to affert, that if the fons of Calas did actually fay there never was a more tender and indulgent father, and that he had never beat one of his children, it is rather a proof of the fimplicity of thofe who believed this depofition, than any mark of innocence in the accufed. It is true, indeed, that it is not an abfolute legal proof; but furely it is highly probable : it was a powerful motive for a further examination, and Mr. Voltaire was only at that time in fearch of fuch circumftances as might determine him to enter thoroughly into this interefting affair, concerning which he afterwards produced fuch convincing proofs, which had been procured for him at Touloufe.

But there is fomething ftill more abfurd. Mr. Voltaire, with whom he paffed three months near Geneva, at the time when he undertook this affair, infifted on it, before he engaged, that Mad. Calas, whom he knew to be a very religious woman, fhould fwear in the name of that God whom fhe adored, that neither her hufband or felf had

L 3   the

the leaſt concern in it. This oath had great
weight, as it was hardly poſſible Mad. Calas ſhould ſwear falſely, or run the hazard of
coming to Paris, and expoſe herſelf to the
ſeverity of the law. She was intirely out of
the cauſe; nothing obliged her to take ſo
dangerous a ſtep as to recommence a criminal proceſs, in which ſhe might have loſt
her life. This author ſeems not to know
how much it muſt ſhock a perſon, with any
ſenſe of religion, to be guilty of perjury;
but this he ſays is a falſe method of reaſoning; " it is juſt as if we were to aſk one of
" the judges who had condemned Calas,"
&c.

But how abſurd is the compariſon! The
judge, no doubt, will make oath, that he
judged according to his conſcience; but
this conſcience might have been impoſed on
by falſe evidence: whereas Mad. Calas could
never be deceived or impoſed on with regard to the crime imputed to her huſband or
herſelf. The accuſed muſt know in their
own hearts whether they were guilty or not;
but

but the judge can only know it by the evidence, which is often equivocal ; the writer
of the paper therefore muſt have argued (for
I love to call things by their names) with as
much folly and malignity.

He makes bold to deny it was ever " be-
" lieved in Languedoc, that the Proteſtants
" make it a point to deſtroy thoſe childien
" whom they ſuſpect of any deſign to change
" their religion." Theſe are the words of
this very ſilly writer. He does not know
that this accuſation was ſo ſeriouſly and ſo
univerſally believed, that Mr. Sudre, the
famous advocate of Touloufe, who gave us
an excellent memorial in favour of the Calas
family, has there refuted this popular error
in page 59, 60, and 61, of his account. He
does not perhaps know likewiſe, that the
church of Geneva was obliged to ſend to
Touloufe a ſolemn proteſt againſt this horrible accuſation.

He makes himſelf merry with this ſerious
and important affair, and laughs at the

L 4   ſcheme

scheme of writing to the governors of Languedoc and Provence, to get proper information from them, that they might know how to proceed. What could have been done better for this purpose?

I shall say nothing of the little witticisms scattered about in this paper. The innocence of Calas, and the solemn decree made by the masters of requests, are things of too much consequence to be debased by the mixture of such trifles.

I ask pardon of Mr. Voltaire for joining his name to that of such a man as Freron; but as these poor and miserable scriblers are suffered at Paris to abuse genius and merit, I thought a soldier, actuated by a sense of honour, might be permitted to speak his sentiments on the occasion; and I am satisfied you may safely impart my thoughts to all lovers of truth.

1

You know how much I am, &c.

LET-

L E T T E R XXXIX.

To the Marquis D'ARGENU.

THE letter you was fo obliging as to
write, fhews at once the goodnefs of your
heart, and the excellency of your underftanding. You acquaint me at this time
with the infolence and bafenefs of Freron,
which I was before a ftranger to, having
never lit of his paper. That chance which
furnifhed you with one of them, was never,
I thank her, fo unkind to me; but you have
extracted gold from his dunghill, by con-
futing his calumnies.

If this man had read the letter which Mad.
Calas wrote from her retreat, where fhe was
almoft expiring, and from whence they
dragged her with the greateft difficulty; if
he had feen the candour, the grief, the refignation, which fhe exprefled in her recital

of

of the murder of her fon and hufband, and
that irrefiftble air of truth with which fhe
called God to witnefs her innocence, he
would not, I believe, have been touched
himfelf, but he muft have feen that every
honeft heart would be touched and convinced alfo.

But tyrants cannot feel the force of nature,
Nor can a Freron feel the pow'r of virtue.

As to marfhal Richelieu, and the duke of
Villars, whofe protection he feems fo much
to undervalue, and whofe teftimony he re-
jects, he does not perhaps know that it was
at my houfe they faw young Calas, whom I
had the honour to prefent to them, and that
moft affuredly they did not protect him till
they had enquired into the affair; after fuf-
pending their judgment a long time, which
every wife man ought to do, before his final
decifion.

As to the mafters of requefts, it is their
bufinefs to fee whether, after their fovereign
deter-

determination, which had confirmed the innocence of Calas and his family, a Freron should be permitted to call it in queſtion.

I embrace, love, and reſpect you,

And am, &c.

L E T-

L E T T E R XL.

To the Abbé de V O I S E N O N.

I Had a little ftunted vine,
Which brought me neither leaves nor wine,
An honeft gard'ner came, and dreft
And trimm'd it fo, that ev'ry gueft
Who us'd to rail at, honour'd me
For my high-flavour'd Burgundy.

I had a rough unpolifh'd ftone,
Which few would deign to look upon;
An artift faw the ufelefs thing,
He cut and form'd it to a ring;
You fee it now a diamond fine,
And brighter than its mafter fhine.

What nature leaves unfinifh'd, art can mend;
Alas! what fhould we do without a friend?

You will eafily guefs, my lord bifhop of
Montrouge, to whom thofe bad verfes are
addreffed.

addreffed. Prefent my compliments to Mr.
Favart, who is one of thofe deities who prefide over the genius of French gaiety. As it
is ten years fince you wrote to me, I dare not
cry out, Write to me, my friend; but I muft
fay, O my friend, you have quite forgotten
me.

L E T-

LETTER XLI.

THE ANSWER.

INgenious Favart, prais'd by thee,
Aſpires to immortality.
On ev'ry bard whom you approve,
Apollo looks with ſmiles of love;
Conſigns the gardens to his care,
And to adorn his patron's hair,
He form'd of flow'rs the choiceſt band
That fell from thy all-pleaſing hand;
As thou art for his maſter known,
He counts thy treaſures as his own.
Whilſt thy example thus the poet fires,
He gives to thee the verſe thy praiſe inſpires.

He would not have failed offering his comedy of Gratitude to you; but he has a ti-
midity natural to men of genius, and feared
it was not worthy of your acceptance. You
will

will hardly believe that, in fpite of all his
merit, the ill-natured world will not allow
him to be the author of his own excellent
works; but malicioufly and unanimoufly attribute half of them to * me. I am fure you

* The public have unanimoufly, fays the
French editor, attributed the moft delicate and
agreeable parts of Mr. Favart's works to M. de
Voifenon; and it muft be acknowledged that
there is a great fimilitude of ftile and manner
between the Annette and Lubin, the three ful-
tanas and the Englifhman at Bourdeaux, and all
the new pieces publifhed by Mr. and Mad.
Favart, with whom Mr. de Voifenon has been
a long time connected. The author of the
Queen of Golconda, Mifapouf, fo much the
worfe for her, and other very agreeable novels,
may very poffibly have compofed love fonnets and
fmart epigrams. It is likewife faid, that Mr.
Favart was not the author of *La Chercheufe
d'Efprit,* a charming little piece, and generally
attributed to the marquis of P—, who is certainly
very capable of writing it.

The prediction in the letter concerning the
Fairy Urgelia was fulfilled. This piece, fo ftrongly talked of, fo warmly defired, and fo highly
applauded at court, was received very coldly at
Paris. In fpite of all the fine habits and decora-
tions beftowed upon it, it did not fucceed at
all.

will

will not fall into this miftake, when he ufes your ftuff to make his holidy cloaths of; you don't make it a point to ftrip him of them.

He will fend you immediately his Fairy Urgelia, which has met with fuccefs at Fontainbleau, which I am juft now come from. This may be no reafon why the piece fhould fucceed at Paris. The court is the chatelet of Paris, and Paris is the grand chamber, which almoft always reverfes its decrees. You indeed furnifhed him with the fubject of this work, which will be its beft recommendation. Adieu, my beft and oldeft friend; I fhall not ceafe to be yours till the parliament fhall recal the Jefuits, nor fhall I ever forget you till I have forgot to read.

LETTER XLII.

To Mr. C A V A I L H A, Author of a Comedy called the TUTOR DUPED, which met with Succefs on the French Theatre.

S I R,   Ferney, Nov. 30, 1765.

I Am greatly obliged to you for the op-portunity you have given me of participating that pleafure which all Paris has tafted in your excellent performance. I am not at all furprized at the fuccefs of it: it has not only in it a variety of pleafing inci-dents, but is fet off by eafy and natu-ral dialogue, and is as well written as played. You will not, I hope, ftop here; but go on to enrich our ftage. It is the

M   greateft

greateſt comfort of my old age to ſee theſe fine arts, which I love, adorned and ſupported by men of ſuch merit and genius.

F I N I S.